JANE EYRE

JANE EYRE

based on the novel by Charlotte Brontë

devised by the original company

OBERON BOOKS
LONDON

WWW.OBERONBOOKS.COM

First published in 2015 by Oberon Books Ltd
521 Caledonian Road, London N7 9RH
Tel: +44 (0) 20 7607 3637 / Fax: +44 (0) 20 7607 3629
e-mail: info@oberonbooks.com
www.oberonbooks.com

A catalogue record for this book is available from the British
Library.

PB ISBN: 9781783199051
E ISBN: 9781783199068

Cover photography by Nadav Kander

Printed, bound and converted
by CPI Group (UK) Ltd, Croydon, CR0 4YY.

Jane Eyre

based on the novel by **Charlotte Brontë**
devised by **the original company**
A **Bristol Old Vic** and **National Theatre** co-production

Cast in alphabetical order
Helen Burns / Adele / Diana Rivers / Grace Poole / Abbot **HANNAH BRISTOW**
Musician **MATTHEW CHURCHER**
Jane Eyre **NADIA CLIFFORD**
Rochester **TIM DELAP**
Musician **ALEX HEANE**
Bertha Mason **MELANIE MARSHALL**
Bessie / Blanche Ingram / St John **EVELYN MILLER**
Mr Brocklehurst / Pilot / Mason **PAUL MUNDELL**
Musician **DAVID RIDLEY**
Mrs Reed / Mrs Fairfax **LYNDA ROOKE**

Understudies
Rochester / Mr Brocklehurst / Pilot / Mason **BEN CUTLER**
Mrs Reed / Mrs Fairfax **JENNY JOHNS**
Bessie / Blanche Ingram / Diana Rivers / Bertha Mason **DAMI OLUKOYA**
Helen Burns / Adele / St John / Grace Poole / Diana Rivers **FRANCESCA TOMLINSON**
Jane Eyre **PHOEBE VIGOR**

Director **SALLY COOKSON**
Set Designer **MICHAEL VALE**
Costume Designer **KATIE SYKES**
Lighting Designer **AIDEEN MALONE**
Music / Music Director **BENJI BOWER**
Sound Designer **DOMINIC BILKEY**
Movement Director **DAN CANHAM**
Fight Director **RENNY KRUPINSKI**
Dramaturg M**IKE AKERS**
Voice and Dialect Coach **KAY WELCH**
Resident Director **HANNAH DRAKE**

OPENING
Lyttelton Theatre 26 September 2017

This production was first staged at Bristol Old Vic in 2014. It transferred to the Lyttelton Theatre at the National Theatre on 17 September 2015 before a short tour including Bristol Old Vic, Nottingham Theatre Royal and Hong Kong Arts Festival.

The 2017 tour opened at the Lowry, Salford on 8 April, then continued to Lyceum, Sheffield; Aylesbury Waterside Theatre; Theatre Royal Plymouth; Mayflower Theatre, Southampton; Festival Theatre, Edinburgh; Grand Opera House, York; New Victoria, Woking; Theatre Royal, Glasgow; Richmond Theatre; Marlowe Theatre, Canterbury; Wales Millennium Centre, Cardiff; Theatre Royal, Newcastle; Milton Keynes Theatre; Norwich Theatre Royal; Theatre Royal, Brighton; Leeds Grand Theatre; Grand Opera House, Belfast; His Majesty's Theatre, Aberdeen; Birmingham Repertory Theatre; and Hull New Theatre.

Bristol Old Vic

Bristol Old Vic is the oldest continuously-working theatre in the United Kingdom, and celebrated its 250th anniversary in 2016. We aim to create pioneering 21st Century theatre in partnership with the people of Bristol, inspired by the history and magical design of our beautiful playhouse.

We originate work in Bristol, which goes on to play on both national and international tour. Most recently, we are delighted to have transferred Peter Pan to the National Theatre, and are thrilled that you are here today to see Jane Eyre.

We are committed to developing the next generation of artists, providing an ongoing programme of opportunity and support through the Bristol Ferment, helping individual artists and companies from across the South West to find and establish their voices as the theatre-makers of tomorrow.

Our award winning Engagement strand creates shows and participatory opportunities for people from all over Bristol and the region, and is currently working with young people from every ward of our city.

In 2016, work began on the final phase of the building's £25m capital development, a long-awaited plan to transform our front of house into a warm and welcoming public space. Designed by Stirling Prize-winning architects Haworth Tompkins, the project is due for completion in Autumn 2018.

Our work connects on a local, national and international level. We are proud to use our funding to support experiment and innovation, to allow access to our programme for people who would not otherwise encounter it, or be able to afford it, and to keep our extraordinary heritage protected and alive.

Chair of the Board **Dame Liz Forgan DBE**
Deputy Chair **Denis Burn**
Chief Executive **Emma Stenning**
Artistic Director **Tom Morris**

Bristol Old Vic, King Street, Bristol, BS1 4ED
0117 987 7877
bristololdvic.org.uk

National Theatre

The **National Theatre** makes world-class theatre that is entertaining, challenging and inspiring. And we make it for everyone.

We stage up to 30 productions at our South Bank home each year, ranging from reimagined classics – such as Greek tragedy and Shakespeare – to modern masterpieces and new work by contemporary writers and theatre-makers. The work we make strives to be as open, as diverse, as collaborative and as national as possible. Much of that new work is researched and developed at the New Work Department: we are committed to nurturing innovative work from new writers, directors, creative artists and performers. Equally, we are committed to education, with a wide-ranging Learning programme for all ages in our Clore Learning Centre and in schools and communities across the UK.

The National's work is also seen on tour throughout the UK and internationally, and in collaborations and co-productions with regional theatres. Popular shows transfer to the West End and occasionally to Broadway. Through National Theatre Live, we broadcast live performances to cinemas around the world.

National Theatre: On Demand. In Schools makes acclaimed, curriculum-linked productions free to stream on demand in every primary and secondary school in the country. Online, the NT offers a rich variety of innovative digital content on every aspect of theatre.

We do all we can to keep ticket prices affordable and to reach a wide audience, and use our public funding to maintain artistic risk-taking, accessibility and diversity.

National Theatre
Box office and information
+44 (0) 20 7452 3000
National Theatre, Upper Ground,
London SE1 9PX
nationaltheatre.org.uk

Registered Charity No: 224223
Registered as a company limited
by guarantee in England: 749504

Jane Eyre was first performed at Bristol Old Vic in 2014 before transferring to the Lyttleton Theatre, National Theatre London 17 September 2015 with the following cast and creative team:

Musician **Benji Bower**
Musician **Will Bower**
Mr Brocklehurst / Pilot / Mason **Craig Edwards**
Helen Burns / Adele / St John / Grace Poole / Abbot **Laura Elphinstone**
Rochester **Felix Hayes**
Musician **Phil King**
Bertha Mason **Melanie Marshall**
Bessie / Blanche Ingram / Diana Rivers **Simone Saunders**
Mrs Reed / Mrs Fairfax **Maggie Tagney**
Jane Eyre **Madeleine Worrall**
Other parts played by members of the company

Director **Sally Cookson**
Set Designer **Michael Vale**
Costume Designer **Katie Sykes**
Lighting Designer **Aideen Malone**
Music / Music Director **Benji Bower**
Sound Designer **Mike Beer** & **Dominic Bilkey**
Movement Director **Dan Canham**
Fight Director **Renny Krupinski**
Dramaturg **Mike Akers**
Company Voice Work **Richard Ryder**
Staff Director **Ellen Havard**

Understudies: Elly Condron (Jane Eyre), Richard Hurst (Rochester/ Brocklehurst/Pilot/Mason), Jools Scott (Musician), Stevie Thompson (Mrs Reed/Mrs Fairfax), Joannah Tincey (Helen Burns/Adele/St John/ Grace Poole/Abbott), Ellena Vincent (Bessie/Blanche Ingram/Diana Rivers/ Bertha Mason)

Act One

A drone.

The musicians and ensemble enter and take positions around the stage. JANE enters alone, walks along the gantry and down the ramp on to the stage. She makes the cry of a newborn baby. She remains on stage watching the rest of the prologue unfold.

The ensemble look on and individually announce the new arrival.

VOICES: It's a girl…it's a girl…it's a girl.

> *The drone builds to a peak. One of the ensemble becomes JANE's MOTHER. The Others turn towards her standing on the platform, holding a bundle of clothes in her arms, representing a baby.*

VOICES: *(All, choral.)* It's a girl!

> *Another ensemble member becomes JANE's FATHER. He climbs up the ladder to join her MOTHER on the platform. They look at the baby adoringly, excited new parents. JANE's MOTHER hands the baby over to the FATHER with great care. He holds her nervously. The baby cries softly.*

FATHER: Jane.

MOTHER: Jane Eyre.

FATHER: Hello.

> *The baby gives another cry. BERTHA begins singing the ballad.*

> > *In the days I went a dancing*
> > *Nor thought of care or woe*
> > *The lads and lasses in their best*
> > *A long time ago*

The parents carry baby JANE down off the platform, across the stage and up the ramp, passing her between them for safety. JANE follows their progress, watching. They move to the gantry. The band begins to play.

As they journey across the stage JANE's father appears to weaken. He begins to collapse very slowly. The ensemble mirror this collapse. The baby cries. He hands the baby over to JANE's mother as he finally falls. JANE moves to be near him as he does so.

JANE's mother is alone with the baby. JANE stands beside her and watches.

AUNT and UNCLE REED put on their costumes and they create a formal picture as the Gateshead portraits fly in. The baby cries and UNCLE REED sets off towards her along the gantry. JANE's mother is collapsing. She hands the baby over to him as she finally falls.

AUNT REED watches from the top of the platform. UNCLE REED brings the baby down the ramp to show her.

UNCLE REED: Hush, little one. You're safe now… You have my sister's nose.

AUNT REED: She'll need a wet nurse.

UNCLE REED: She shall have a wet nurse.

AUNT REED: What a sickly looking little thing.

UNCLE REED: She's beautiful. Call the children.

AUNT REED: Eliza! Georgiana! John!

The children gather around AUNT REED on the platform, looking down at UNCLE REED as he gazes at the baby. BERTHA sings.

UNCLE REED: Children, meet your cousin Jane. You are to think of her as your sister.

The children look uncertainly at AUNT REED. She comes down from the platform and joins UNCLE REED. He takes her hand, impressing on her what she must do.

UNCLE REED: Sarah. You must look after her. She is family.

He hands AUNT REED the baby, lifts the trap door. BERTHA holds it open for him.

UNCLE REED: Promise me you will take care of her…
Promise me!

AUNT REED: I promise.

The children come down from the platform and gather round AUNT REED as UNCLE REED descends under the stage, closing the trap as he goes. AUNT REED holds the baby at arm's length. As the music reaches a crescendo she shakes out the bundle and it becomes the dress that JANE will wear. As BERTHA finishes singing the ballad, AUNT REED strides across to where JANE is standing and roughly pulls the dress over her head and does up the buttons. JANE is a child now, living with her cousins at Gateshead.

> *The mountains stand before me*
> *The rivers running wild*
> *The wind it howls the rain it falls*
> *Upon this orphan child*

JANE stands awkwardly in her dress on one side of the stage. The Reed family are gathered opposite, regarding her with suspicion. They look out to the audience as the scene ends.

SCENE ONE
JANE CLASHES WITH JOHN REED

A clap of thunder, the sound of heavy rain falling. AUNT REED calls to the children.

AUNT REED: Children, come in quickly. John, Georgiana, Eliza, hurry!

They gather with AUNT REED on the ramp.

AUNT REED: Oh my darlings, you're soaked. Come and sit by the fire. Get yourselves dry. I'll have Bessie bring some hot milk and cinnamon buns. Bessie? Bessie?

The children go up the ramp as if going inside. AUNT REED follows, looking for BESSIE. Music. JANE is alone under the platform. She swings on it aimlessly, lost in thought. AUNT REED returns looking for BESSIE and is surprised to discover JANE.

AUNT REED: Bessie!? Jane? Why are you in here? You were supposed to be outside with the other children. Well? Have you anything to say for yourself?

JANE: What have I done Aunt Reed?

AUNT REED: I do not like questioners, Jane. Until you learn to behave like a happy, contented child then I must exclude you from the privileges enjoyed by the others. Tiresome child, off with you... Go on. Bessie?! Where are those buns?

AUNT REED leaves. JANE goes to her sanctuary on the platform and finds a book.

JANE: Bewick's History of British Birds.

She leafs through the pages.

JANE: Northern diver...osprey...cormorant....arctic tern.... The arctic tern haunts solitary rocks and promontories, where the Atlantic surge pours into the arctic zone, that reservoir of frost and snow, where firm fields of ice surround the pole and its death white realms....its death white realms. The little bird hovers over the ice and skims across the dark ocean waves...flap...flap...flap.

JOHN REED calls out to JANE from the ramp. She tries to sneak away down the ladder, but he runs across to the platform and stands on a stool so that he can see JANE trying to get away.

JOHN: Rat!... Rat! There you are Rat!

JANE: What do you want?

JOHN: Say 'What do you want *Master Reed.*'

JANE: What do you want Master Reed?

JOHN: I want you to come down.

JANE does as she has been instructed and comes down from the platform. He sits on the bottom of the ramp observing her. JOHN points to show exactly where he would like her to stand.

JOHN: Come here. Stand here.

He jumps up and grabs her hair.

JOHN: What have you been doing?

JANE: Reading.

He reaches up on to the platform and gets the book.

JOHN: This is my book. You have no business reading *my* book. All these books belong to me. Everything here will be mine when the old girl dies. You have nothing. You have no money. Your father left you none. You ought to beg, not live here with gentlemen's children like us. I'll teach you to go rummaging around in my bookshelves. Come and stand over here. I don't want to break anything.

JOHN points to where he wants JANE to stand. She follows his orders. JOHN carefully takes aim with the book as JANE stares at him. The whole of the ensemble mime the throwing of the book. There is a loud crack and JANE collapses with a cry. JOHN chuckles to himself and makes his way under the platform.

JANE: You vicious cruel pig. You're like a murderer. You're like the Roman emperors!

JOHN is outraged and returns.

JOHN: What did you call me?

JANE: Vicious fat pig!

JOHN: You called me a pig?

JANE: Yes!

JOHN goes for JANE. She leaps on him, scratching and biting wildly. JOHN falls on the floor, trying to crawl away as JANE continues to hit him.

JOHN: Mother! Mother!

JANE bites JOHN. He screams in agony. AUNT REED calls for assistance from the gantry and then moves to the platform. BESSIE and MISS ABBOT rush in and grab JANE, pulling her off the stricken JOHN.

AUNT REED: Bessie! Abbot! Come quickly! Jane is trying to murder Master John!

JOHN escapes, running up the platform.

AUNT REED: Oh you poor thing, come to me, come on.

JOHN: She bit me mother!

AUNT REED: She has bitten him! Jane…you are no better than an animal. Take her away to the Red Room and lock her in.

BESSIE and ABBOT stand on the ramp looking down at JANE as JOHN and MRS REED disappear. They move her to a stool centre stage, as the scene transforms to the Red Room.

SCENE TWO
THE RED ROOM

JANE is forced to sit on a stool by the platform. Her resistance is weakening.

BESSIE: Sit still and be quiet. For shame Miss Eyre! What shocking conduct. Biting a young gentleman! Your young master!

JANE: Master? How is he my master? What am I? A servant?

BESSIE: No. You are less than a servant, for you do nothing for your keep. Now sit still and do not stir. Or God will punish you. He might strike you down in this very room, just as he did your Uncle Reed. He died in here. You should repent or something bad might come down the chimney and get you.

ABBOT and BESSIE leave. JANE sits in silence for a moment in the eerie light. The ensemble create a door at the top of the ramp. JANE gets up and runs over to it, pulling at the handle in vain before hammering on it four times.

JANE: Unjust! Unjust!

JANE gives up on the door and walks back down the ramp towards the stool. A flash of light scares her. She has caught a glimpse of her own reflection in a mirror.

JANE: It's just a mirror. Why am I always accused? I strive to fulfill every duty, yet still they call me naughty and tiresome and sullen and sneaking. It's unjust.

JANE returns to the stool and sits down feeling utterly dejected.

JANE: Ow...my head... Uncle Reed. If you were here you would have been kind to me.

BERTHA sings from the top of the platform.

> You're cold in the ground
> Worms thread through your bones
> As you lie in your earthly grave

A drone rises towards a crescendo. UNCLE REED's ghost appears from the trap, holding the bundle of clothes as if it were a baby. JANE starts to panic.

JANE: No! Uncle Reed! Please stay away! Please don't come here. Let me out! Let me out! Please! Help!

JANE is on the ramp tugging at the door. BESSIE appears at the top of the ramp.

JANE grabs hold of her leg, begging for help.

BESSIE: Miss Eyre? Are you ill? What a dreadful noise, it went right through me.

JANE: I saw a light and I thought a ghost had come.

AUNT REED appears at the top of the platform.

AUNT REED: What is all this? Bessie, I believe I gave orders that Jane Eyre was to be left in the Red Room till I came to her myself.

BESSIE: But she screamed out so loud mam.

AUNT BESSIE: She has screamed on purpose. I know her tricks. Loose Bessie's leg, child. You cannot succeed in getting out by these deceitful means, be assured. You will now stay in here an hour longer.

JANE rushes across to the ladder and begins climbing up towards AUNT REED.

JANE: No. Aunt Reed. Please. Please, have pity on me. Have mercy. Have mercy.

AUNT REED: Silence! This violence is almost repulsive. Bessie! Lock the door!

AUNT REED and BESSIE leave. As the lights black out we hear the sound of the door slamming shut.

SCENE THREE
BESSIE COMFORTS JANE

As the lights come up one of the band sings a reprise of the ballad over the action.

In the days I went a dancing
Nor thought of care or woe
The lads and lasses in their best
A long time ago

JANE sits at the bottom of the ramp feeling miserable. BESSIE puts a blanket round her shoulders and then moves the stool to the side of the stage. They walk up the ramp together, along the gantry and on to the platform. BESSIE begins busily folding a basket of washing. JANE slumps against the ladder staring into the distance.

BESSIE: It's right nice outside you know… John and the girls have gone out… I know! I can go and get one of those books.

JANE continues staring.

BESSIE: Come on Miss Jane, cheer yourself up. When's all this going to end? All this crying, it will do you no good.

JANE: I cry because I am miserable Bessie.

BESSIE: Miserable? You've nowt to be miserable for. Mrs Reed has done you a great service taking you in. You ought to be thankful for your good fortune.

JANE: It's unjust.

BESSIE: You should learn to keep your passions under control. Try to think of good things.

BESSIE sits down next to JANE.

JANE: There are no good things.

BESSIE: I don't know what's to be done with you. You will end up in the poorhouse. How would you like that?

JANE: I shouldn't like to be a beggar and have no shoes and no fire.

BESSIE: I've heard Mrs Reed is making enquiries about sending you to school.

JANE: School?

BESSIE: Do you remember those young ladies I told you about in the last family I worked for? They went to school. They could embroider. And translate from the French.

JANE: And play piano? And paint watercolours?

BESSIE: And most importantly they learned how a young lady should behave. It's not easy mind you. They have backboards to make you sit up straight and if you don't do as you're told you get the slipper.

JANE: I shouldn't mind the punishment if it were fair.

BESSIE: Perhaps school will suit your temper then. Now come here and make yourself useful.

They continue folding the washing together.

SCENE FOUR
THE INTERVIEW WITH BROCKLEHURST

MR BROCKLEHURST walks along the gantry wearing a large top hat.
AUNT REED sits in a chair doing needlework. As BROCKLEHURST
arrives at the bottom of the ramp, JANE is standing in front of the
platform.

AUNT REED: This is the little girl whom I should like you to
find a place for.

BROCKLEHURST: Her size is small. What is her age?

AUNT REED: Ten years.

BROCKLEHURST: So much? And what is her parentage?

AUNT REED: She is an orphan. Her father was a clergyman.
He died of an infection whilst living amongst the poor.
Her mother, my husband's sister, followed soon after.
That is the price you pay for marrying below yourself.

BROCKLEHURST: What is your name, girl?

JANE: Jane Eyre, sir.

BROCKLEHURST: Well, Jane Eyre. Are you a good child?

JANE is silent. BROCKLEHURST beckons her to come closer.

BROCKLEHURST: Come here.

JANE approaches him.

BROCKLEHURST: Do you know where the wicked go after
death?

JANE: To hell, sir.

BROCKLEHURST: And what is hell?

JANE: A burning pit of fire.

BROCKLEHURST: Should you like to fall into that pit and be
forever burning?

JANE: No, sir.

BROCKLEHURST: Than what must you do to avoid it?

JANE: I must keep in good health and not die, sir.

BROCKLEHURST: And how will you do that? Children younger than yourself die daily. I buried a child of five years old only a day or two since – a good little girl, whose soul is now in heaven. It is to be feared the same could not be said of you should you be called hence. Do you read your Bible?

JANE: Sometimes.

BROCKLEHURST: Are you fond of it?

JANE: I like Revelation and the Book of Daniel and Genesis and Samuel and a little bit of Exodus, and some parts of Kings, and Chronicles and Job and Jonah.

BROCKLEHURST: And the Psalms? I hope you like them?

JANE: The Psalms are not interesting.

AUNT REED: Mr Brocklehurst, should Jane be admitted to Lowood I would ask that the staff there all guard against her worst fault: a tendency to deceit.

BROCKLEHURST begins circling around her.

BROCKLEHURST: Deceit? Deceit is indeed a sad fault in a child. All liars will have their portion in the lake burning with fire and brimstone. She shall be watched.

AUNT REED: I wish her to be brought up in a manner suiting her prospects, to be made useful and to be kept humble.

BROCKLEHURST: Plain fare, simple attire, unsophisticated accommodations, hardy and active habits. Such is the order of the day at Lowood.

AUNT REED: I will send her as soon as possible. As for the vacations she will, with your permission, spend them always at Lowood.

BROCKLEHURST: That request can be accommodated ma'am. Little girl, here is a book entitled 'A Child's Guide.' I penned it myself. Read it with daily prayer, especially 'An account of the awfully sudden death of Martha, a child addicted to falsehood and deceit…
The house awoke to a deathly cry
As the devil choked Martha on her lie.' *(To AUNT REED.)* Good day.

BROCKLEHURST leaves, going up the ramp and along the gantry.

AUNT REED: Return to the nursery.

JANE begins to leave but then turns and marches back to confront AUNT REED.

JANE: I am not deceitful. If I were I would say I loved you; but I declare I do not love you. This book about the liar you may keep it yourself, for it is you who tells lies, not I.

AUNT REED: What more have you to say?

JANE: I am glad you are no relation of mine. I will never call you aunt again as long as I live. I will never come to see you when I am grown up and if anyone ever asks me how I liked you, and how you treated me, I will say the very thought of you makes me sick and that you treated me with miserable cruelty.

AUNT REED: How dare you affirm that Jane Eyre!

JANE: How dare I Mrs Reed? How dare I? Because it is the truth. You think I can do without one bit of love or kindness, but I cannot live so. I shall remember how you thrust me back into the Red Room to my dying day; though I was in agony; though I cried out while suffocating with distress. And that punishment you made me suffer because your wicked boy knocked me down for nothing. Send me to school soon Mrs Reed, for I hate to live here.

AUNT REED: I will indeed send you to school Jane Eyre. I will indeed.

AUNT REED goes up the ramp and exits. JANE follows her for a moment, then she turns, sits under the platform and buries her head in her hands.

SCENE FIVE
JANE AND BESSIE GOODBYE

JANE is slumped down on the ramp in tears. BESSIE climbs up on to the platform looking for her, calling to her as she goes.

BESSIE: Miss Jane? Miss Jane! Miss Jane!

She calls for a third time as she reaches the bottom of the platform. JANE stands up and BESSIE sees her.

BESSIE: You naughty little thing. Why don't you come when you're called?

JANE: Come Bessie, don't scold.

A member of the ensemble brings in JANE's coat. BESSIE takes it, helps JANE to put it on and then inspects her.

BESSIE: The coach is on its way. Are you ready? Let me look at you. Are you sure you've washed your face? Did you do behind you ears?

JANE: Get off.

The ensemble have entered. One of them hands BESSIE a small package, which she hands on to JANE.

BESSIE: Dinner. Make sure you eat it all *(Another package is handed to BESSIE.)* Tea. Keep it safe. Will you go in and bid Missis goodbye?

JANE: She came in to my room last night and she said I need not disturb her in the morning and that I was to remember that she had always been my best friend and to speak of her and be grateful to her accordingly.

BESSIE: And what did you say?

JANE: Nothing. I hid beneath the bedclothes and turned my face to the wall.

BESSIE: That was wrong Miss Jane.

JANE: It was quite right Bessie. Your Missis has not been my friend; she has been my foe.

BESSIE: How coolly my little lady talks. I dare say now if I were to ask you for a kiss goodbye you wouldn't give it to me.

JANE: I'll kiss you and welcome. Bend your head down.

JANE stands and BESSIE bends her head down. JANE kisses the top of her head.

BESSIE: Come here.

BESSIE stands and hugs JANE.

BESSIE: Now you work hard at that school. Goodbye Miss Jane.

A drum beat begins.

JANE: Goodbye Bessie.

BESSIE exits.

SCENE SIX
JOURNEY TO LOWOOD

JANE picks up her bag and walks to the centre of the stage.

JANE: Goodbye box hedge. Goodbye gravel path. Goodbye wet lawn… Goodbye Gateshead!!

On the count of four a stronger rhythm kicks in. The ensemble gather around JANE, playing other passengers in the coach. When the rhythm kicks in they all begin running on the spot.

BAND: First stop Sherriff Hill, Ayton Banks, Lamesley, the beautiful Birtley, Painshaw, Waldridge, Lumley, Kimblesworth, Burwin Gate, Greydale, Durham.

The ensemble spread out across the stage and begin sprinting on the spot as the rhythm changes to double time.

BAND: Ferry Hill, Merrington, Windlestone, Blackwell, Hurworth, Stanwick, Allerton, Topcliffe, Sandhutton, Asenby, Richmond, Bedale, STOP!!

COACHMAN: Right ladies and gentlemen. Widdle break.

The ensemble scatter and find a place to go to the toilet. They are all very relieved.

COACHMAN: Right, shake a peg and down your leg, let's get back on't' road!

There is another four count and the rhythm begins again. The ensemble reassemble in the centre of the stage. One of them is almost left behind.

PASSENGER: Hey! Wait for me!

BAND: Next stop Flaxby, Leathley, Eccleshill, Churwell. Woh!!

The rhythm stops.

COACHMAN: What the bloody heck's this?

The ensemble transform into a flock of sheep. They circle around JANE.

COACHMAN: Get them animals out of the road! Come on sheep, we haven't got all day.

The sheep disappear as the ensemble re-form around JANE. The band make a final four count and the rhythm kicks in again, the ensemble running asleep as if the coach journey is going on long into the night. One by one they exit during this final section, until an exhausted JANE is running by herself.

BAND: Next stop Langthorpe, Arkendale, Ripon, Stanley, Skelton, Hornby, Ouse Burn, Dishforth, last stop Lowood.

The rhythm slows and stops, leaving JANE alone in a spotlight.

SCENE SEVEN
ARRIVAL AT LOWOOD

The ensemble become staff at Lowood. A voice calls out from the darkness.

VOICE: Is there a little girl called Jane there? Jane Eyre from
Gateshead?

JANE: Yes.

> *The ensemble enter and begin busying themselves around her. One
> of them takes her bag. The others examine her hair etc as part of the
> admissions procedure.*

VOICE: Follow me child.

VOICE: The child is very young to be sent alone.

VOICE: She looks tired. She should be sent to bed.

VOICE: Are you tired child?

JANE: A little mam.

VOICE: Is this the first time you've left your parents to come to
school?

JANE: I don't have any parents.

VOICE: How long have they been dead?

JANE: Since I was a baby.

VOICE: And how old are you now?

JANE: Ten years old.

VOICE: Can you read and write and sew a little?

JANE: Yes, mam.

> *The ensemble pull JANE's Gateshead dress over her head.*

VOICE: Then I hope you will be a good child. Give her some
supper before she goes to bed.

VOICE: Biscuit.

VOICE: Cup of water.

VOICE: Blanket.

JANE is given a biscuit, a cup of water and a blanket. Her uniform is thrown down at her feet.

VOICE: Here is your uniform. You must wear it at all times during your residence here.

ALL: Good night child.

SCENE EIGHT
LIFE AT LOWOOD

JANE stands alone in a spotlight, wrapped in a blanket. BERTHA begins singing 'Kyrie'. The lights come up and the ensemble enter carrying their Lowood uniforms. BROCKLEHURST appears at the top of the ladder above the platform and begins preaching from there.

BROCKLEHURST: Lowood Institution for the education and edification of poor, orphaned and abandoned girls.

The Lowood students mime washing in freezing cold water.

BROCKLEHURST: Blood of my savior bathe me in thy tide
Wash me in the waters gushing from thy side.
Come you children, let me teach you the fear of God. Keep your tongue from evil and your lips from speaking lies.

The Lowood students cough in rhythm with the underscore.

BROCKLEHURST: God's eyes are towards the righteous.
His ears listen to their cries.
Many are the afflictions of the righteous but God will deliver you out of them all.

The Lowood students get into their uniforms and put on their bonnets. Church bells ring. They form into a group underneath the platform. The students sing a chorus of 'Kyrie'. The music changes. The students travel along the gantry and back down the ramp until they are standing directly beneath BROCKLEHURST.

BROCKLEHURST: What is God?

STUDENTS: God is the supreme spirit.

BROCKLEHURST: Where is God?

STUDENTS: God is everywhere.

BROCKLEHURST: What is sin?

STUDENTS: Sin is an offence against God.

BROCKLEHURST: What was the sin committed by Eve?

STUDENTS: The sin committed by Eve was the sin of temptation.

BERTHA begins a chorus of 'Kyrie'. The ensemble join in. At the end of the chorus they move in front of the platform where they recite a prayer in unison.

ALL: O my God
   Because you are so good
   I am very sorry that I have sinned
   By the help of your Grace
   I will not sin again
   I will not sin again (x2)

BROCKLEHURST recites the catechism over this. The music finishes.

BROCKLEHURST: What is sin? Sin is an offence against God.

VOICE: Girls! File out!

BROCKLEHURST exits. The students move over to the ramp and stand around the edge. One of the ensemble becomes a TEACHER. JANE waits by the platform.

TEACHER: You may be seated.

The students all sit, except for HELEN Burns.

TEACHER: Eyre, come and sit here behind King. Burns, stop daydreaming.

JANE and HELEN both sit.

TEACHER: Thread your needles and knot the tail end, we are
doing blanket stitch, a quarter of an inch from the edge.
Sit up straight, King!

*The teacher slaps King round the head. The ensemble vocalize the
sound.*

ALL: Slap!

TEACHER: Sloppy work, Bower. Take it out and start again.

The TEACHER stands over HELEN who has not started sewing yet.

TEACHER: Burns! Focus on the task in hand!

The TEACHER slaps HELEN.

ALL: Slap!

The ensemble exit.

SCENE NINE
JANE MEETS HELEN

HELEN is reading. JANE sits down next to her on the platform.

JANE: Is your book interesting?

HELEN: I like it.

JANE: What's it about?

HELEN: You may look at it.

HELEN passes the book to JANE.

JANE: What is your name besides Burns?

HELEN: Helen.

JANE: Do you come from a long way from here?

HELEN: I come from a place farther north quite on the borders
of Scotland.

JANE: Will you ever go back?

HELEN: I hope so. But nobody can be sure of the future.

JANE: Why is this place called Lowood Institution? Why not Lowood School?

HELEN: Well we're all charity children. All the girls here have lost either one or both parents and this is called an Institution for educating orphans.

JANE: Do they keep us for nothing?

HELEN: Our families pay fifteen pounds a year.

JANE: Fifteen pounds? So why do they call us charity children?

HELEN: Because fifteen pounds is not enough. And the rest is paid by generous ladies and gentlemen of Mr Brocklehurst's parish.

JANE: So you are an orphan?

HELEN: My mother is dead.

JANE: How long have you been here?

HELEN: Two years.

JANE: Are you happy here?

HELEN: You ask rather too many questions. I have given enough answers for the present. Now I want to read.

HELEN gets up and takes her book back. She exits.

SCENE TEN
HELEN PUNISHED

The ensemble stand in a row, heads bowed. One of them becomes the TEACHER.

TEACHER: Thus concludes our chapter on the execution of King Charles the First. Who was listening?

Everyone raises their hand.

TEACHER: Let's see shall we? When was King Charles executed?

One hand goes up.

TEACHER: Hayes?

STUDENT: 1649, mam.

TEACHER: Vague. More detail.

Another hand.

TEACHER: King?

STUDENT: January mam…uh…

TEACHER: If you don't know the answer, don't put your hand up.

HELEN puts her hand up.

TEACHER: Burns?

HELEN: Tuesday January 30th 1649 mam.

TEACHER: And where was he executed?

HELEN: Outside the banqueting hall at the Palace of Whitehall mam.

TEACHER: And what were his final words?

HELEN: Therefore I tell you that I am a martyr of the people. I have a good cause and a gracious God on my side.

The TEACHER grabs HELEN's hands and inspects them.

TEACHER: Eyre. Fetch the rod from the cupboard.

JANE fetches the rod.

TEACHER: Burns, you dirty, disagreeable girl. You never scrubbed your fingernails this morning.

The TEACHER marches HELEN to the top of the ramp. The ensemble look on and make the sound of the rod swishing through the air as

HELEN is beaten. The TEACHER *places a sign saying 'slattern' around* HELEN's *neck.*

TEACHER: Hardened girl. Nothing can correct your slatternly habits.

The teacher exits up the ramp and the students follow.

SCENE ELEVEN
HELEN AND JANE (2)

HELEN sits at the foot of the platform with her book. JANE enters.

JANE: Is it the same book?

HELEN: Yes and I have just finished it.

JANE: You must wish to get away from this place.

HELEN: Why should I? I was sent to Lowood to get an education and it would be of no use going away until I have attained that object.

JANE: But that teacher was so cruel to you.

HELEN: Not at all. She is severe. She dislikes my faults.

JANE: I should resist her if she struck me with that rod. I should get it from her and break it under her nose.

HELEN: Probably you would do nothing of the sort, but if you did, Mr Brocklehurst would expel you.

JANE: You say you have faults Helen, what are they? To me you seem very good.

HELEN: We are all burdened by faults in this world. Learn from me not to judge by appearances. I am, as the teacher said, slatternly. I seldom put and never keep things in order. I am careless. I forget rules. I read when I should learn my lessons.

JANE: It is curious. It is so easy to be careful.

HELEN: For you I have no doubt that it is. Your thoughts never seem to wander. Mine continually rove away. Sometimes I think I am in Northumberland and the noises I hear are the sound of a bubbling little brook that runs through Deepden near our house and when it comes to my turn to reply, I have to be wakened and I have no answer ready. This is all very provoking to the teacher who is naturally neat, punctual and particular.

JANE: And cross and cruel. And you're so good Helen.

HELEN: Yes, in a passive way, but there is no merit in such goodness.

JANE: Yes there is. You are good to those who are good to you. If you are good to all those who are cruel, the wicked people would have it all their own way. So we should strike back.

HELEN: No. I cannot believe that. I hold another creed, which no one ever taught me and I seldom mention, but in which I delight and cling to. With this, revenge never worries my heart and injustice never crushes me too low.

JANE: I don't understand.

A STUDENT runs down the ramp looking for HELEN.

STUDENT: Helen Burns if you don't go put your drawer in order and fold up your work this minute, I'll tell Miss Scatcherd to come and look at it!

HELEN: Love your enemies Jane and bless them that curse you.

HELEN gets up and exits.

SCENE TWELVE
JANE PUNISHED

The ensemble become the Lowood students again and form a group centre stage.

Music plays as they shiver in front of a meager fire. They move into a line and recite their night prayers.

VOICE: How should you finish the day?

ALL: I should finish the day by kneeling down and saying my prayers.

VOICE: After your night prayers what should you do?

ALL: After my night prayers I should observe due modesty in going to bed, occupy myself with thoughts of death and endeavor to compose myself to rest at the foot of the cross and give my last thoughts to my crucified saviour.

They all fall asleep, leaning on each others' shoulders. The music ends.

BROCKLEHURST appears on the ramp carrying a pile of books and he gives them out to the line of students as he speaks.

BROCKLEHURST: My plan in bringing up you girls is not to accustom you to habits of luxury and indulgence but to render you hardy, patient and self-denying. I have been informed that there have been occasions when the porridge has been burnt. This should not be seen as the spoiling of a meal, but an opportunity to muse on the sufferings of the early Christian martyrs.

JANE drops her book.

BROCKLEHURST: Careless girl. Let the child who dropped her book step forward. Ah, Jane Eyre. I have a few words to say regarding you.

The other students take a step back so that JANE is alone. BROCKLEHURST walks towards JANE.

BROCKLEHURST: *(To one of the students.)* Stool.

The STUDENT gets a stool from off stage and places it next to JANE.

BROCKLEHURST: Place yourself on it child.

JANE sits on the stool.

BROCKLEHURST: No. I wish you to stand.

JANE stands on the stool as the other students file out, up the ramp and on to the platform.

BROCKLEHURST: You all see this girl? My dear children,
I must warn you that this little girl is a castaway, not of
the true flock but evidently an interloper and an alien.
You must be on your guard against her. You must shun
her example, avoid her company, exclude her from your
sports, for this girl is a servant of the evil one! This girl...is
a liar! Let her stay on the stool and let no one speak to her
for the remainder of the day.

BROCKLEHURST exits up the ramp. The students file out. HELEN glances up at JANE as she passes. JANE is left standing on the stool, alone. BERTHA sings.

> *My feet they are a weary*
> *My limbs they are sore*
> *I have travelled across this land so far*
> *How long I can't be sure*

SCENE THIRTEEN
HELEN AND JANE (3)

HELEN enters from under the platform with a piece of bread. She offers it to JANE standing on the stool.

HELEN: Here. Eat it.

JANE stares ahead and doesn't take the bread. HELEN sits down at the foot of the stool. Silence for a moment. JANE gets down from the stool.

JANE: Why do you stay with a girl who everybody believes to
be a liar?

33

HELEN: Everybody? Eighty girls heard you so called and the world contains hundreds of millions.

JANE: I cannot bear to be solitary and hated. To have some real affection from you or anyone I truly loved I would willingly submit to have the bone in my arm broken, or let a bull toss me, or to stand behind a kicking horse and let it dash its hoof at my chest....

HELEN: Shh Jane, you think too much of the love of human beings. If the whole world hated you while your own conscience absolved you from guilt, you would not be without friends.

HELEN offers the bread again and JANE accepts. HELEN breaks it and they eat together.

SCENE FOURTEEN
HELEN'S DEATH

The ensemble become the Lowood students and take up positions around the stage. HELEN and JANE become part of the group.

Music. The ensemble wash themselves in freezing water and cough in rhythm as they count off the passing months.

ALL: November... December... January... February...

March, March, April... May... June, June... June.

HELEN is under a blanket and sitting on the edge of the platform.

JANE: How is Helen Burns?

TEACHER: She is very poorly child.

JANE: What did the doctor say when he came?

TEACHER: We must all pray for her.

JANE: May I go and see her?

TEACHER: No child. The sick bay is out of bounds.

JANE thinks for a moment, then climbs up the ladder to the platform to see HELEN.

JANE: Helen? Are you awake?

HELEN: What are you doing here, Jane? It is past eleven o'clock.

JANE: I came to see you Helen. I heard you were very ill.

HELEN: You came to bid me goodbye then.

JANE: Are you going home?

HELEN: Yes, to my last home.

JANE: No!

HELEN: Jane, it's cold. Come and cover yourself with the quilt. I'm very happy Jane. And when you hear that I am dead you must be sure and not grieve. There is nothing to grieve about. We must all die some day and the illness that is removing me is not painful.

JANE: Where are you going Helen? Can you see?

HELEN: I am going to God.

JANE: Where is God? What is God?

HELEN: Besides this Earth there is an invisible world and a kingdom of spirits. It's everywhere and those spirits watch us.

JANE: So will I see you again Helen, when I die?

HELEN: You will come to the same region of happiness no doubt.

JANE: Does it exist?

HELEN: I feel as if I could sleep. But don't leave me Jane. I like to have you near me.

JANE: I'll stay with you.

HELEN: Are you warm?

JANE: Yes.

HELEN: Good night Jane.

JANE: Good night Helen.

They fall asleep. The ensemble form a choir and sing 'Christ With Me.' HELEN gets up and climbs down the ladder. One of the ensemble opens the trap and HELEN exits through it. The trap closes. The lights come up. JANE carefully folds HELEN's blanket. She climbs down the ladder. She kneels by the trap and places her hand on it.

SCENE FIFTEEN
JANE BECOMES AN ADULT

Music. JANE lifts her arms and a member of the ensemble lifts her school dress over her head. Another ensemble member hands her a corset, which she puts on. On the gantry another ensemble member is waiting with her petticoats.

She steps into them and moves to the platform. The ensemble gather around her and help her into her adult dress. She ties her hair into a bun. Once she is dressed, the ensemble become her pupils.

JANE: Good morning children. My name is Miss Eyre and I will be your teacher here at Lowood.

Music. JANE teaches the ensemble.

JANE: Encore une fois.

ALL: Je suis, tu es, il est, elle est, nous sommes, vous etes, ils sont, ells sont.

JANE: Tres bien. Encore une fois.

STUDENT: 1649.

JANE: And what were the final words of the King? Saunders?

STUDENT: Therefore I tell you that I am the martyr of the people. I have a good cause and gracious God on my side.

JANE: Encore une fois.

ALL: Je suis, tu es, il est, elle est.

One of the ensemble holds up a wooden square which becomes a small window. There is a pause in the music. JANE stares out of this small window. The moment breaks, the window disappears and we return to the lessons.

JANE: Very good Edwards. Please don't wipe your nose on your sleeve. It is a bit cold in here though isn't it? Now thread your needles and tie a knot at the tail end, we're doing blanket stitch, a quarter of an inch from the edge. Encore une fois.

ALL: Je suis, tu es, il est, elle est, nous sommes, vous etes, ils sont, elles sont.

Another member of the ensemble offers a window to JANE. The music pauses. She stares out of the window before the moment breaks and the window disappears.

JANE: Encore une fois.

The ensemble begin a cacophony of repetition continuing the rote learning of the French with snippets of the other lessons coming in over the top. As they are doing so, they create a large window from the smaller individual ones at the front of the platform. JANE looks out of it.

JANE: Enough!

JANE breaks the window apart with a gesture. She looks longingly into the distance.

JANE: There are the two wings of the school building. There is the gate. There is the road that cuts into the gravel track. And beyond, the blue peaks, the blue peaks. Those blue peaks.

The window re-forms in front of JANE.

JANE: I must have liberty. And if I cannot have liberty then let me have change. Grant me at least a new servitude. Think!

The window disappears. JANE travels along the gantry on to the ramp. The ensemble sit on the edge of the platform. They have become her inner voices.

JANE: Think! Think! Think!

VOICE: What can I do?

JANE: I can get a new place. With new people, under new circumstances. Why do I want this?

VOICE: Because it is of no use wanting anything better.

VOICE: How do people get a new place?

JANE: They apply to friends I suppose.

VOICE: I have no friends.

VOICE: Plenty of people have no friends.

JANE: What do they do?

ALL: Advertise…as a governess.

JANE: I must advertise in the Yorkshire Herald.

The ensemble exit, leaving MRS FAIRFAX standing on the platform.

FAIRFAX: To JE who advertised in the Herald last Thursday, a situation can be offered her where there is but one pupil, a little girl under ten years of age. The salary is thirty pounds per annum.

The ensemble help JANE to get her bag and coat. They give her food for the journey.

VOICE: Dinner.

FAIRFAX: JE is requested to travel at her earliest convenience.

VOICE: Tea.

FAIRFAX: Mrs Fairfax, Thornfield Hall.

The journey rhythm begins, the ensemble gather around JANE.

JANE: Goodbye Lowood.

The band do a four count and the ensemble begin running with JANE as before.

The Lowood dresses are flown out.

BAND: First stop Rockwith, Bramhope, Methley, watch
   your back, Ragby, Moston, Royston, Matlock, Butterby,
   Turnditch, Mackworth, Lubley, Millcote, woah!!!

COACHMAN: Bloody English weather! Sorry love, you'll have
   to get out and walk. There's too much ice on't lane. But
   Thornfield Hall is just down the way.

SCENE SIXTEEN
ENCOUNTER WITH ROCHESTER

*Drums, tinkling horse brass and music accompany ROCHESTER's
entrance. He clings on to the ladder on the side of the platform, which
is his horse. His dog PILOT, runs around barking uncontrollably. As
the music ends, ROCHESTER falls off his horse and hurts his leg. He
lies on the ground, furious with himself. JANE looks on.*

ROCHESTER: Ow! Fuck! Fuck! Fuck it!

JANE: Are you injured sir?

ROCHESTER: Stand back!

JANE tries to help again.

ROCHESTER: Just stand to one side.

The horse gets up.

JANE: Is there anything I can do to help?

ROCHESTER: Just be on your way!

*ROCHESTER tries to get up but collapses again. PILOT continues
barking around him.*

ROCHESTER: Pilot! Pilot!

JANE: I cannot think of leaving you alone in this solitary lane
   at such a late hour unless I see you are fit to mount your
   horse.

ROCHESTER: Necessity compels me to make you useful. Come here.

JANE goes across to him and helps him up.

ROCHESTER: Turn! You have to turn!

He leans on her and is finally able to hobble across to his horse.

ROCHESTER: Woah! Easy, easy, easy. There you go.

He climbs back on to the horse with difficulty. JANE picks up his crop and passes it to him. PILOT circles around her.

ROCHESTER: I'm obliged to you. Pilot, away! You're not lost?

JANE: No.

ROCHESTER: You know where you're going?

JANE: Yes, thank you.

ROCHESTER: Well, good evening.

JANE: Good evening.

ROCHESTER and PILOT exit. BERTHA sings a verse of the ballad.

> *The mountains stand before me*
> *The rivers running wild*
> *The wind it howls the rain it falls*
> *Upon this orphan child*

SCENE SEVENTEEN
ARRIVAL AT THORNFIELD

JANE walks along the gantry with her luggage. The ensemble gather on the platform. JANE emerges from underneath, arriving at Thornfield Hall.

JANE: Hello?

MRS FAIRFAX appears at the top of the ramp and comes down to greet JANE.

FAIRFAX: Jane Eyre? How do you do? Oh aren't your poor hands cold. Welcome to Thornfield.

JANE: Mrs Fairfax?

The ensemble light the way into Thornfield with hand held lamps. They create a fire. JANE warms herself in front of it.

FAIRFAX: Yes indeed. Come and stand by the fire, get yourself warm. Let me take your coat. Can I get you anything? Something to eat perhaps?

JANE: No thank you.

FAIRFAX: What a journey you must have had! All that way in the frost and the snow. I am glad you are come. Sometimes one can feel very alone rattling around these empty corridors of a night time.

ADELE calls down from the top of the platform.

ADELE: C'est elle ma gouvernante?

JANE: Bonjour. Tue es encore debout?

ADELE: Vous parlez Francais!

FAIRFAX: Adella! You are supposed to be asleep!

ADELE: Je ne suis pas fatigue Madame Fairfax.

FAIRFAX: Off to bed with you now!

ADELE: Jusqu'a demain, mademoiselle.

ADELE exits.

JANE: She's French.

FAIRFAX: She has a few words of English but I have the devil of a job to get her to use them. You must be exhausted. Let me show you to your room.

Music. MRS FAIRFAX picks up JANE's bag and begins escorting her to her room. The ensemble light the way with the hand held lamps.

FAIRFAX: Thornfield is a fine old hall though very much neglected of late in Mr Rochester's absence.

JANE: Who is Mr Rochester?

FAIRFAX: He is the owner. Did you not know?

JANE: I thought Thornfield belonged to you?

FAIRFAX: To me? Bless you child, what an idea. I am only the
    housekeeper.

JANE: And the child? My pupil?

FAIRFAX: Adella is Mr Rochester's ward. He brought her
    over from France at the end of last summer. Such a shame
    he spends so much time on the continent. Great houses
    require the presence of their proprietors.

They arrive at JANE's room.

FAIRFAX: Here we are my dear. I do hope you'll be
    comfortable. I've put you in one of the smaller rooms. The
    large apartments at the front are so sombre. The fire's kept
    in. Good. Good.

JANE looks around the room.

FAIRFAX: Your window overlooks the garden. Go up on to
    the battlements tomorrow, it's a wonderful view. There is
    Rochester land as far as the eye can see.

JANE: Is Mr Rochester well respected?

FAIRFAX: He is a good master. Somewhat peculiar perhaps,
    though not strikingly so. My bedroom is along the corridor,
    just knock if you need anything. Good night Miss Eyre.

SCENE EIGHTEEN
THE LAUGH

*Birdsong. JANE is exploring Thornfield next morning. She walks along the
gantry to the ramp. The ensemble create a large window at the bottom.
JANE pushes it open and leans out. The wind makes her dress flap behind
her. The window snaps shut again. JANE hears strange noises, among
them BERTHA singing. She goes back the way she came to investigate.
She hears a laugh and rushes back feeling spooked.*

JANE: Mrs Fairfax! Mrs Fairfax!

FAIRFAX: Good morning my dear. What is it?

JANE: I heard something. Like a laugh.

FAIRFAX: Probably one of the servants. Grace Poole very
    likely.

JANE: Did you hear it?

FAIRFAX: I often hear her. She sews in one of the rooms on the
    third floor. She sometimes has one of the maids in to assist
    her. They can be very noisy together.

GRACE POOLE walks along the gantry. MRS FAIRFAX calls to her.

FAIRFAX: Too much noise Grace. Remember directions.

GRACE exits.

FAIRFAX: Now it's time to meet your pupil properly. As Miss
    Adella's governess you will be responsible for teaching her
    all the accomplishments expected of a modern young lady.
    Improving her English is a priority, but she must also be
    able to dance, do fine needlework and play piano. In the
    evenings, after she is in bed you may sit with me in the
    parlour. On Sundays we all attend church together.

SCENE NINETEEN
TEACHING ADELE

*JANE is on the platform, ADELE stands on the ladder as the first lesson
begins.*

JANE: Now then, Adele, in our lessons we will always speak in
    English. We'll start with numbers...

ADELE: Je ne comprends pas.

JANE: We'll start with numbers and then move on to simple
    nouns, like animals.

ADELE: Parlez en Francais!

JANE: Then we will combine them as follows: one cat, two
    dogs, three pigs and so on.

ADELE: Je ne comprends pas!

JANE: One, two, three, four, five…

ADELE: *(Mocking her.)* Un, deux, trois, quatre, cinq…

JANE: I see you do understand.

ADELE: En Francais.

JANE: English.

ADELE: En Francais!

JANE: English.

ADELE: En Francais!!

JANE: Oh well, never mind, we'll try again another day.

ADELE and JANE move from the platform to the stage. Time has passed.

The sound of a flock of geese flying overhead.

ADELE: Goose.

JANE: Geese.

ADELE: Much goose.

JANE: Many geese.

ADELE: Many geese. Honk honk.

JANE: Well done Adele.

They move to another part of the stage for a history lesson.

ADELE: Les derniers mots du roi furent 'J'ai une bonne cause et un Dieu bienvellant de mon côté.'

JANE: Tres bien.

MRS FAIRFAX enters.

FAIRFAX: I cannot understand a word she says when she runs on so.

ADELE: I am learning the kings of England.

FAIRFAX: History? What does a young girl need with that?

They move again, sitting on the ramp doing needlework.

ADELE: Must we do sewing again?

FAIRFAX: What else would a young lady do of an evening?

One of the band sings 'Who Stole Your Crown.'

> *She was young, wild fire eyes a-gleaming*
> *Lost on the Western wind*
> *By the hands of love she was bound and blinded*
> *To her final end*

> *Who stole your crown?*
> *While your back was turned*
> *Bow your head down*
> *While your body slowly burns*

JANE, ADELE and MRS FAIRFAX change positions four times whilst sewing. Finally ADELE is frustrated.

ADELE: I cannot do it. I have made a knot again.

JANE: Give it to me.

ADELE thrusts her sewing at JANE and walks out. MRS FAIRFAX follows her.

FAIRFAX: She is tired. I will see to her. Another day done.

The ensemble become JANE's inner voices.

VOICE: I should be happy.

JANE: I know I should.

VOICE: I should be content.

VOICE: Adele is a good pupil.

VOICE: Mrs Fairfax has a kind heart.

JANE: I know.

VOICE: I should not be restless.

JANE: It is in vain to say human beings ought to be satisfied with tranquility. We must have action.

VOICE: Women are supposed to be very calm, generally.

JANE: Women feel just as men feel. They need exercise for their faculties and a field for their efforts as much as their brothers do. Must I confine myself to making puddings and embroidering cushion covers? I wish to exercise my mind. I wish to be allowed freedom.

BERTHA is heard laughing. GRACE POOLE scurries across the platform and down the ladder. JANE sees her and they briefly meet.

GRACE: Miss.

GRACE exits. PILOT runs in and goes straight up to JANE, barking. JANE strokes him.

MRS FAIRFAX enters.

FAIRFAX: Miss Jane you'll have to see to Adella yourself. The master has returned without a word of warning, his bed's not made up and cook's got nothing in.

PILOT is sitting in ROCHESTER's armchair.

JANE: Is this Mr Rochester's dog?

FAIRFAX: Yes and he's a blooming nuisance. Pilot! Out! Come on! Master wants to see you and Adele in the drawing room tomorrow after dinner.

MRS FAIRFAX and PILOT exit.

SCENE TWENTY
ROCHESTER AND JANE (1)

JANE calls ADELE over and tries to make her look smart ready for MR ROCHESTER's arrival. She tidies her up and wipes her face. PILOT comes back in and sits in the chair wagging his tail. ADELE sits on the floor next to the chair and JANE stands beside her. ROCHESTER marches in down the ramp.

ROCHESTER: You?

FAIRFAX: May I introduce Miss Eyre.

JANE: Good evening, sir.

ROCHESTER: You're Adele's governess?

JANE: Yes sir.

FAIRFAX: Do you know each other?

ROCHESTER: Yes Mrs Fairfax. This woman leapt out at me on Hay Lane and felled me from my horse.

JANE: I hope there were no bones broken, sir.

ROCHESTER: Pilot! Out!

PILOT moves to the floor. ROCHESTER sits in the armchair.

ADELE: Bon soir, Monsieur Rochester.

ROCHESTER: It's good evening Adele. Good evening, not bon soir. You're not in bloody Paris any more.

ADELE: Good evening, Mister Rochester.

ROCHESTER: Better.

ADELE: Excuse me, sir, est ce que vous avez un cadeau pour moi? Et pour Miss Eyre aussi?

ROCHESTER: No, I have not brought you a present. Miss Eyre, are you fond of presents?

JANE: I believe they are generally thought pleasant things.

47

ROCHESTER: Generally thought? What do you think?

JANE: I have very little experience of them, sir.

ROCHESTER: You are more sophisticated than Adele. She demands a present. You beat about the bush.

JANE: That is because she has greater confidence in her deserts than I have.

ROCHESTER: Don't fall back on over modesty! I have examined Adele. She is not bright, she has no talents and yet Mrs Fairfax tells me that in short time she has made much improvement.

JANE: There, sir. You have now given me my cadeau. It is the mead teachers most covet: praise of their pupil's progress.

ROCHESTER: Humbug! *(ROCHESTER goes upstage to get a drink.)* Have a seat Miss Eyre. *(JANE sits down with MRS FAIRFAX at the bottom of the gantry.)* You have been in my house for three months? Where did you come from?

JANE: Lowood institution.

ROCHESTER: Who are your parents?

JANE: I have none.

ROCHESTER: So were you waiting for your people as you sat on that stile?

JANE: For whom, sir?

ROCHESTER: The men in green. When you leapt out at me I thought unaccountably of fairy tales. Did I break through one of your fairy rings, that you spread that damned ice on the causeway?

JANE: The men in green all forsook England a hundred years ago, sir and not even in Hay Lane or the fields about it might you find trace of them. I don't think either summer or harvest or winter moon will ever shine on their revels more.

ROCHESTER: Adele showed me your portfolio this morning. *(He fetches the portfolio and begins leafing through it.)* Were these paintings all your own work? Probably a master aided you.

JANE: No indeed.

ROCHESTER: Ah, that pricks pride. Where do your ideas come from?

JANE: From my head.

ROCHESTER: From that head I see on your shoulders?

JANE: Yes.

ROCHESTER: They are weird. The thoughts are elfish. Were you happy when you painted these?

JANE: As happy as I have ever been, sir.

ROCHESTER: Put the drawings away. *(He brusquely hands the portfolio to JANE.)* What are you about, Miss Eyre? It's gone nine o'clock. Take Adele to bed.

JANE: Adele, come.

ADELE: Bon nuit.

JANE: Good evening, sir.

ADELE, JANE and PILOT exit up the ramp. ROCHESTER remains in his armchair. JANE stops MRS FAIRFAX on the gantry.

JANE: You said Mr Rochester was not strikingly peculiar, Mrs Fairfax.

FAIRFAX: Well, is he?

JANE: He seems very changeful and abrupt.

FAIRFAX: I am so used to his manner I never think of it. If he has peculiarities of temper, allowance should be made.

JANE: Why?

FAIRFAX: He has painful thoughts that make his spirits unequal.

JANE: What about?

FAIRFAX: Family troubles.

JANE: I thought he had no family.

FAIRFAX: Not now, but he has had. He broke with them long ago, some misunderstanding with his father. Mr Rochester is not very forgiving.

SCENE TWENTY-ONE
TIME PASSES AT THORNFIELD

JANE and ADELE climb up on the platform. ADELE recites her two times table in English. ROCHESTER is in his armchair below, watching. He gets up and calls PILOT to follow him. ADELE completes her tables.

ADELE: One times two is two, two times two is four etc.

JANE: Well done Adele, that will do for today.

JANE and ROCHESTER pass each other near the ladder.

JANE: Sir?

ROCHESTER: I see you can count as well as paint, Miss Eyre.

JANE: You have discovered my only other talent.

ROCHESTER: Modesty again? I thought we had done away with that.

JANE: Old habits are hard to break.

JANE watches ROCHESTER as he sits on the end of the ramp staring wistfully into the distance. He moves away with PILOT. JANE paces in front of the platform, ROCHESTER watching her.

SCENE TWENTY-TWO
ROCHESTER & JANE (2)

ROCHESTER calls down from the platform.

ROCHESTER: Adele! Adele!

ADELE enters.

ADELE: Oui?

ROCHESTER: I have something for you!

ADELE: Quoi? La boite? C'est pour moi?

ROCHESTER: Yes. Take it away and disembowel it, but do it quietly.

ROCHESTER hands a gift box down to ADELE.

ADELE: Merci, Mr Rochester. Merci! Merci pour mon cadeau!

ROCHESTER: Mrs Fairfax, take her to the nursery and make sure that she doesn't bother me.

FAIRFAX: Yes, sir.

ADELE moves to the gantry and sits down to open her present, escorted by MRS FAIRFAX. PILOT follows her. ROCHESTER comes down from the platform to his chair. He indicates to JANE where he wants her to sit.

ROCHESTER: Miss Eyre, pull up your chair. No, not there. Here! Here! *(ROCHESTER fetches a drink. They sit together in a slightly awkward silence.)* You examine me, Miss Eyre. Do you think me handsome?

JANE: No, sir.

ROCHESTER: There is something singular about you. You sit there sewing away in silence and then you come out with a comment like that.

JANE: Please forgive me sir, I was too plain.

ROCHESTER: Yes, you were.

JANE: I should have said something like beauty is of little consequence.

ROCHESTER: You should have said no such thing. Find fault with me.

JANE: It was a blunder.

ROCHESTER: Yes it was. And you shall answer for it. Criticise me. Does my forehead not please you? *(JANE is not sure how to respond.)* You look puzzled Miss Eyre. And while you are no more pretty than I am handsome a puzzled air becomes you. So puzzle on... I am disposed to be gregarious and communicative tonight. We are going to have a conversation. Now speak.

JANE: What about, sir?

ROCHESTER: Anything you like.

Silence.

ROCHESTER: You are dumb, Miss Eyre. Stubborn. And now annoyed.

JANE: I am willing to amuse you, if I can sir, but how will I know what will interest you? You ask me questions. I will do my best to answer them.

ROCHESTER: Fine. But as I've roamed half the globe while you've lived quietly in a corner, don't I have a right to be somewhat masterful, abrupt even, without you being piqued by my tone of command?

JANE: Do as you please, sir.

ROCHESTER: That is no answer.

JANE smiles.

ROCHESTER: The smile is very well, but speak too.

JANE: I was merely thinking sir, that few masters would concern themselves as to whether or not their paid subordinates were piqued by their tone of command.

ROCHESTER: Paid subordinates? I pay your salary, don't I? Well, on that mercenary ground, if I dispense with many conventional forms and phrases, will you think their omission arises from insolence?

JANE: I should never mistake informality for insolence, sir: one I rather like, the other, nothing freeborn would submit to, even for a salary.

ROCHESTER: Humbug. Most things freeborn would submit to anything for a salary. Perhaps you are an exception. I don't mean to flatter you Miss Eyre. It is no merit of yours. Nature did it. You may yet prove to have intolerable defects to counterbalance your few good points.

JANE: We are all burdened by faults in this world, sir.

Pause.

ROCHESTER: I was set on the wrong path at the age of twenty-one and have never recovered the right course since. On the whole nature meant me to be a good man. I am not. Not that I am a villain, just a sinner. A trite commonplace sinner. You must wonder that I tell you this? You have a peculiar mind. You listen with an innate sense of pity.

ADELE charges in to show off her new dress.

ADELE: Qui est belle? Merci pour ma belle robe! C'est tres bien! Qu'est ce que je suis magnifique! Tut comme maman!

ROCHESTER: Adele! Get out Adele! Mrs Fairfax I told you to keep her out.

FAIRFAX: I'm sorry sir, she runs so fast!

ROCHESTER: Pilot! Out! Out! Go on!

ROCHESTER chases PILOT out of the room. ADELE continues to be in view, dancing in her room on the platform.

ROCHESTER: Do you think she resembles me?

JANE: I could not say sir.

ROCHESTER: I have a past existence. A series of deeds that I daily regret. Dread remorse when you are tempted to err, Miss Eyre. Remorse is the poison of life.

JANE: Repentance is said to be its cure, sir.

ROCHESTER: Her mother insisted she was mine. I see no proof in her countenance. Pilot is more like me than she is. Celine Varens was her name. An opera dancer. She abandoned the child and ran away with a singer. You have never felt jealousy have you? I need not ask because you have never felt love. Now you know the child is a French dancer's bastard, you will perhaps think differently of your position here?

JANE: Not at all, sir. Now I know she was forsaken by her mother and disowned by you, I shall cling more closely to her than before.

ROCHESTER: I like this night. I like Thornfield, its old crow trees. The lines of dark windows. How long have I hated the very thought of this place? Shunned it like some great plague house. I will like it! I dare like it! I will break any obstacles to happiness, to goodness, I wish to be a better man than I have been, than I am…. You listen as if it were the most natural thing in the world for a man like me to tell tales of his opera mistress to a young governess. I see at intervals the glance of a curious sort of bird through the close-set bars of a cage. A vivid, restless, resolute captive is there. Were it but free, it would soar, cloud high. You fear me because I talk like a sphinx.

JANE: No, sir, I am certainly not afraid.

ROCHESTER: Good night, Miss Eyre.

ROCHESTER exits.

SCENE TWENTY-THREE
JANE REFLECTS

The ensemble become JANE's inner voices, gathering round the armchair.

JANE: That was an unexpected evening. He talked a lot.

VOICE: A lot.

VOICE: He talked.

VOICE: He talked a lot to me.

JANE: Why?

VOICES: Why? Why? Why?

JANE: He said I was a good listener.

VOICE: I am a good listener.

JANE: I think he was just drunk.

VOICES: I think he was drunk/He was on the brandy/Did you
see how much was left in the bottle?/Half a bottle

JANE: But he did say I have a peculiar mind.

VOICE: Is that good?

VOICE: Peculiar's good.

VOICE: Is peculiar good?

VOICE: No. Peculiar's not good.

JANE: He's peculiar.

VOICES: He's very odd/He is peculiar.

JANE: I will like it. I dare like it.

SCENE TWENTY-FOUR
THE FIRE

Sinister music. The lights dim. ROCHESTER lies down in his bed on the ramp, covered in a blanket, the ensemble around him. BERTHA enters under the platform, singing.

> *Deep in the burning ice*
> *Lies a flame*
> *Deep in the burning ice*
> *Lies a flame*

BERTHA strikes a match. The ensemble create the fire around ROCHESTER's bed by striking matches into fire buckets. Strange sounds awaken JANE. She looks out along the gantry.

JANE: Who's there? Who's there?

Flames begin to rise out of the buckets and JANE realises there is a fire. She races down the ladder to ROCHESTER's bedside.

JANE: Sir! Sir, wake up! Sir! Get out of bed, sir. Sir!

ROCHESTER wakes up and together they beat out the flames with the bed sheets.

The ensemble leave.

JANE: Sir, I heard someone laughing in the corridor. Someone has tried to hurt you. Shall I fetch Mrs Fairfax?

ROCHESTER: Mrs Fairfax? No, she'd wake the entire house. Jane, I have to leave you for a few moments. If you're cold, take my coat.

JANE: Shall I come with you, sir?

ROCHESTER: No. Stay here. Do not move or call anyone until I return.

ROCHESTER heads up the ladder and across the platform on to the gantry. He meets GRACE POOLE there. A brief whispered conversation takes place before he returns.

ROCHESTER: I have found it all out. It is exactly as I thought. The laughter in the corridor...you have heard it before I should think?

JANE: Yes sir. There is a woman that sews on the third floor. Grace Poole. She laughs in that way.

ROCHESTER: Grace Poole. Just so.

JANE: She is strange sir, I don't think you should have her in the house, she is not to be trusted.

ROCHESTER: You are no talking fool, Jane. Say nothing more about it. You ought to go to bed.

JANE: Good night then, sir.

ROCHESTER: You are leaving me already?

JANE: You said I might go, sir.

ROCHESTER: You save my life and then walk away as if we were mere strangers. At least shake me by the hand.

They shake hands.

ROCHESTER: I have the pleasure of owing you an immense debt.

JANE: There is no debt sir, there is no obligation of any kind.

ROCHESTER doesn't let go.

JANE: I'm glad I happened to be awake. Good night again, sir.

JANE extricates herself from ROCHESTER and she exits.

SCENE TWENTY-FIVE
AFTER THE FIRE

JANE enters on to the platform, still carrying ROCHESTER's dressing gown. GRACE is clearing the bedroom after the fire, collecting buckets and carrying them out. A look between them as GRACE moves up the ramp.

JANE: Good morning Grace.

GRACE: Miss.

JANE: A strange affair.

GRACE: Indeed Miss. *(She goes to leave, but hesitates and decides to speak further to JANE.)* May I ask, are you in the habit of bolting your door at night?

JANE: I am not. I was not aware there was any danger at Thornfield. In future I shall make sure my door is locked securely before I venture to lie down.

GRACE: It may be wise to do so, Miss.

GRACE exits as MRS FAIRFAX enters. She is also mopping up after the fire.

FAIRFAX: If I've said it once I've said it a thousand times, it is dangerous to keep a lighted candle by your bedside. It is a wonder the master was not killed. I do hope you take heed Jane. I know you are fond of reading in bed. I only hope we can restore the place to order before Mr Rochester returns.

JANE: Is Mr Rochester gone somewhere?

FAIRFAX: He has gone to Lord Ingram's, on the other side of Millcote.

JANE: But you expect him back tonight?

FAIRFAX: No, he's likely to be away a week or more. Quite a party is assembling there. The Ingrams and the Eshtons. Colonel Dent. And Blanche Ingram will be coming of course. Lord Ingram's eldest.

JANE: What's she like?

FAIRFAX: She's a real beauty. She came here one Christmas when she were about eighteen. Sang a duet with Mr Rochester, voice of an angel.

JANE: I was not aware he could sing.

FAIRFAX: He only sings in the company of other ladies and gentlemen. If there is a better match for him anywhere in the county I have yet to hear about it.

MRS FAIRFAX takes ROCHESTER's dressing gown from JANE and exits.

SCENE TWENTY-SIX
THE INGRAMS ARRIVE

JANE paces the ramp. She tries to get on to the platform, but the ensemble block her way as they become the self-critical voices in her head. They climb on to the platform and surround her.

VOICE: You, a favourite with Mr Rochester?

VOICE: You, gifted with the power of pleasing him?

VOICE: You, of importance to him in any way?

JANE gets to the platform. The ensemble follow her there.

VOICE: Well open your eyes and look at yourself.

VOICE: It is madness in all women to let a secret love kindle within them.

VOICE: Listen then Jane Eyre and look.

The ensemble hold up their mirrors. JANE circles, looking into each one of them and seeing herself as she is perceived by society, plain and poor.

VOICE: Draw in chalk your own picture without softening one defect.

VOICE: Write under it.

VOICE: Portrait of a governess, disconnected, poor and plain.

VOICE: Now take a piece of the finest parchment.

VOICE: Paint carefully the loveliest face you can imagine.

JANE: Write under it 'Blanche Ingram: an accomplished lady of rank.'

VOICE: When ever in future you should chance to fancy that Mr Rochester thinks well of you…

VOICE: Take out these pictures and compare them.

BERTHA begins singing as JANE sketches a picture of herself in chalk on the platform. She sings 'Mad about the boy' by Dinah Washington.

> *Mad about the boy*
> *I know it's stupid to be mad about the boy…*

The ensemble leave and JANE carries on sketching alone on the platform.

JANE: A more fantastic idiot than Jane Eyre has never lived.

The Ingram party appears on the gantry. A soundscape and movement section capturing the atmosphere of their arrival at the house. At the end of this sequence BLANCHE and ROCHESTER become animated.

BLANCHE: Edward, you will sing and I shall play for you.

ROCHESTER: A command from you Blanche, I am all obedience.

ADELE hears them and runs out excitedly into the space.

ADELE: Enchante mademoiselle.

BLANCHE: Who is this?

ROCHESTER: May I introduce my ward, Adele Varens.

BLANCHE: What a poppet of a child.

ROCHESTER: And her governess, Miss Eyre.

JANE comes out from under the platform.

JANE: Sir.

BLANCHE: I must have had half a dozen governesses when I was a child. You should send this girl to school.

ROCHESTER: I have not considered the subject.

BLANCHE: You men never do. Are you in good voice tonight Signior Eduardo?

ROCHESTER: Signior Eduardo? You make me sound like a Spanish mercenary.

BLANCHE: A Spanish mercenary would suit me fine.

ROCHESTER and BLANCHE exit.

SCENE TWENTY-SEVEN
MASON ARRIVES

ROCHESTER and BLANCHE move to the gantry. They are silhouetted, deep in conversation. JANE moves from under the platform to the bottom of the ramp, observing ROCHESTER and BLANCHE. She watches for a moment then turns away. As JANE walks away from the party gathering she meets MASON entering.

MASON: Pardon me madam, for the late hour. I am an old friend of Mr Rochester's. I was hoping to see him.

JANE: He is in the drawing room. He has guests. Shall I take you to him?

MASON: No. I have no wish to break up the party. If you would be so kind as to inform him that Mr Mason is here. From Spanish Town in Jamaica.

JANE: I'll fetch him, sir.

As JANE returns centre stage she meets ROCHESTER coming in the opposite direction.

ROCHESTER: Good evening Jane.

JANE: Good evening, sir.

ROCHESTER: How do you do?

JANE: Very well thank you.

ROCHESTER: Why did you not come and speak to me in the drawing room?

JANE: I did not wish to disturb you sir, as you seemed engaged.

ROCHESTER: And what have you been doing during my absence?

JANE: Teaching Adele as usual.

ROCHESTER: You didn't catch cold that night you dragged me out of bed?

JANE: Not the least.

ROCHESTER: Return to the drawing room, you are deserting too early.

JANE: I am tired, sir.

ROCHESTER: And a little depressed.

JANE: I am not depressed. There is a man who's come to see you. I have left him in the hall. His name is Mason.

ROCHESTER staggers.

JANE: Sir? Sir? Are you ill, sir?

JANE goes over to him.

ROCHESTER: I wish I were on a quiet island with only you. Trouble and danger on the far side of the world.

JANE: What can I do?

ROCHESTER: Where is he?

JANE: In the hall.

ROCHESTER gets up. MASON enters.

ROCHESTER: Richard!

MASON: Edward.

They greet each other and hug.

ROCHESTER: Let's get a drink. Warm you up!

They exit.

SCENE TWENTY-EIGHT
MASON ATTACKED

The ensemble are gathered on the ladders, watching BERTHA and MASON circling each other underneath the platform. BERTHA suddenly strikes at him and he screams.

ROCHESTER: Jane? Are you up?

JANE: Yes, sir.

ROCHESTER: You must come with me. To the third floor.

They travel along the gantry.

ROCHESTER: You don't turn sick at the sight of blood?

JANE: I don't think so.

They come down the ramp and discover MASON covered in blood.

ROCHESTER: How are you Mason?

MASON: She's done for me I fear.

ROCHESTER: Bear up man! You thought you were dead as a herring a moment ago, now you're all up and talking.

MASON: She bit me. She worried me like a tigress when you took the knife off her.

ROCHESTER: I warned you not to visit her without me.

MASON: I thought it might do some good.

ROCHESTER: Well it hasn't, has it? You're not dying. I will go for the surgeon.

MASON: And what of her?

ROCHESTER: What more would you have me do? Jane, try to stop the bleeding. Under no circumstances will you speak to this man. Richard, you talk to her on peril of your life. Do you understand? Can I rely on you, Jane?

JANE: Yes, sir.

A linking voiceover section.

ROCHESTER: *(V/O.)* Mason. Mason! The surgeon's here.

MASON: *(V/O.)* The fresh air revives me.

ROCHESTER: *(V/O.)* Open the windows on his side.

MASON: *(V/O.)* You must take care of her. Treat her as tenderly as may be.

ROCHESTER: *(V/O.)* I do my best. I have done it and I will do it.

The sound of the horse and carriage pulling away.

SCENE TWENTY-NINE
IN THE THORNFIELD GARDEN

Bird song. ROCHESTER and JANE in the garden.

ROCHESTER: You've passed a strange night Jane

JANE: Yes, sir.

ROCHESTER: Mason will be half way to Liverpool by now.

JANE: And the danger you spoke of sir: Is that gone too?

ROCHESTER: Not until he is out of the country. Perhaps not even then.

JANE: Grace Poole must be sent away. Your life is at risk while she remains.

ROCHESTER: To live, for me Jane, is to stand on the crater crust, which may crack and spew fire at any time.

JANE: Then speak to Mason. Tell him he must avert the danger.

ROCHESTER: Jane! Suppose that you were a wild indulged boy in a foreign land. There you commit a capital error. Mind I do not say crime. My word is error. Over time the results of what you have done become utterly insupportable. You are desperate. You seek happiness in heartless, sensual pleasures. Finally you come home. You make a new acquaintance. You find in this stranger all the bright qualities you have sought for twenty years and you feel better days come back. You wish to recommence your life. To attain this end are you justified in overleaping a mere conventional impediment?... Is this man justified in daring the world's opinion in order to attach himself forever to this gentle stranger?

JANE: A sinner's reformation should never depend on a fellow creature, sir. If anyone you know has suffered or erred, let him look higher than his equals for strength and solace.

ROCHESTER: But the instrument! The instrument! God, who does the work, ordains the instrument. I believe I have found the instrument for my cure...little friend, you may perhaps have noticed my penchant for Miss Ingram. Don't you think that if I married her she would regenerate me with a vengeance? You look quite pale Jane. You must curse me for disturbing your rest.

JANE: Curse you? No, sir.

They stand and shake hands.

ROCHESTER: Shake my hand in confirmation of the word. You have cold fingers. When will you watch with me again?

JANE: Whenever I might be useful, sir.

ROCHESTER: Perhaps the night before I am married. I am sure I will not be able to sleep. Will you promise to sit up with me and talk of my lovely one? To you I can talk of her, for you have seen her and you know her.

JANE: Yes, sir.

ROCHESTER: She's a rare one, is she not Jane?

JANE: Yes, sir.

ROCHESTER: She's a strapper, she's a real strapper. The house will be awake soon. You'd best go in by the shrubbery.

ROCHESTER exits. The ballad 'Poor Orphan Child' reprises. BERTHA enters and stands on the ramp, she looks up at JANE as she sings the first verse solo.

> In the days I went a dancing
> Nor thought of care or woe
> The lads and lasses in their best
>
> A long time ago

The ensemble enter the space and join in with the song.

> A breeze did blow the blossom down the green
> Leaves died away
> The echoing cry of a crow on the wing
> Told me I could not stay

JANE collapses in tears slumped next to the ladder.

> My feet they are a weary
> My limbs they are a sore
> I have travelled across this land so far
> How long I can't be sure
>
> The mountains stand before me
> The rivers running wild
> The wind it howls the rain it falls
> Upon this orphan child

End of Act One.

Act Two

SCENE ONE
THE MAELSTROM

A drone.

The ensemble are scattered across the stage as the lights come up, running on the spot. JANE runs with them. A soundscape of voices – memories from JANE's past – begins.

MAELSTROM SOUNDSCAPE: Care for her Sarah. Promise me!

What a sickly looking little thing.

You must learn to keep your passions under
control.

Take her to the Red Room and lock her in.

For shame Miss Eyre.

Unjust.

I must have liberty.

Is Mr Rochester well respected?

You – you're Adele's governess!

Blanche Ingram, she's a rare one is she not Jane?

If there's a better match for him anywhere in the county I
have yet to hear of it.

You've never felt jealousy have you Miss Eyre? I need not
ask, because you've never felt love.

Are you in good voice tonight Signor Eduardo?

I must have liberty.

Unjust! Unjust!

I will like it! Wake up!

I dare like it!

Wake up!

The ensemble freeze.

JANE: Do something.

SCENE TWO
JANE ASKS FOR LEAVE

BLANCHE and ROCHESTER enter, looking around the grounds.

BLANCHE: Edward! Edward!

VOICES: *(All.)* Do something!

BLANCHE: This is the ideal spot for a climbing rose.

ROCHESTER: Is it Blanche? I'm sure you are right. You are after all a font of botanical knowledge.

JANE: Mr Rochester?

BLANCHE: Edward, the governess is hovering again. What does that creeping creature want now?

ROCHESTER: Go up to the house, I shan't be a moment.

BLANCHE: Well do hurry.

BLANCHE exits.

ROCHESTER: Well, Miss Eyre?

JANE: If you please sir, I've received a letter. My aunt is very ill. I've decided I would like to visit her.

ROCHESTER: Your aunt? I thought you said you had no relations.

JANE: None that would own me sir.

ROCHESTER: I trust this will be a fleeting visit. Promise me to stay no more than a week.

JANE: I will not make a promise I might be obliged to break.

ROCHESTER: You will need money. You cannot travel without money. How much have you in the world?

JANE: Five shillings. You have not yet given me my salary, sir.

ROCHESTER: How much do I owe you?

JANE: I have been here six months, so you owe me fifteen pounds.

ROCHESTER takes a fifty out of his wallet.

ROCHESTER: Here.

JANE: This is fifty pounds, sir. You owe me fifteen.

ROCHESTER: I do not want change. Take your wages.

JANE: I will not take more than I'm owed.

ROCHESTER takes the fifty back and looks in his wallet again.

ROCHESTER: Fine. What have I got? *(He finds a ten.)* There. Ten. That is plenty.

JANE: Yes, but now you owe me five.

ROCHESTER: You will have to come back to Thornfield to collect the balance.

ROCHESTER goes to leave.

JANE: Mr Rochester, there is another matter of business I should like to discuss while I have the opportunity.

ROCHESTER: A matter of business?

JANE: You have as good as informed me that you are shortly to be married. In that case, Adele ought to go to school and I must seek another situation.

ROCHESTER: We will talk about this when you return.

JANE: No, sir. Now. I shall advertise.

ROCHESTER: At your peril you advertise. Give me my ten pounds back Jane, I have a use for it.

JANE: No, sir. Not five shillings nor five pence.

ROCHESTER: Jane! Promise me not to advertise. Leave the question of your future employment to me.

JANE: Only if you in turn promise that Adele and I will both be safe out of the house before your bride enters it.

ROCHESTER: Very well. I give you my word.

JANE: Thank you sir.

JANE heads down the platform on her way out.

ROCHESTER: I shall see you after supper as usual?

JANE turns to him. The ensemble mirror her.

JANE: I shall be packing.

ROCHESTER: Then I will have to rely on someone else to keep me amused.

BLANCHE appears.

BLANCHE: There you are Edward. They're serving drinks in the drawing room.

JANE: Goodbye sir.

JANE exits. ROCHESTER and BLANCHE watch her leave. ROCHESTER heads down the ramp, calling PILOT as he goes. PILOT follows them out.

SCENE THREE
RETURN TO GATESHEAD

The journey rhythm begins again as the scene transforms to Gateshead.

BAND: First stop Butterby, Topcliffe, Blackwell, Gateshead.

The rhythm slows to a halt. BESSIE is sitting under the platform folding washing. Her son BOBBY is studying next to her. JANE enters down the ramp. BESSIE gets up to greet her.

BESSIE: Jane? Jane Eyre!

JANE: Bessie.

BESSIE: Well look at you. *(They embrace.)* You're a proper young lady now aren't you? Give me your coat. Sit down.

JANE: You look very well.

BESSIE: Thank you. Married life must be good for me.

JANE: You're married?

BESSIE: Yes. To Robert. You remember…the coachman. Got two little ones as well. That's Bobby over there. Say hello Bobby.

BOBBY: Hello.

JANE: Hello, Bobby.

BESSIE: So, you're a governess. I always knew you had it in you. I bet they taught you an awful lot at that school of yours. I bet you speak French.

JANE: Yes Bessie, I can both read it and write it.

BESSIE: Bobby loves languages. Say something in French to him. Go on.

JANE: No, Bessie.

BESSIE: Go on. Bobby! Miss Jane's going to say something to you, in French.

JANE and BESSIE go across to BOBBY. JANE kneels down next to him.

JANE: Bonjour Bobby. Qu'est'ce que tu lis? Est-ce qu'il y a beaucoup d'images?

BESSIE: Say something back.

BOBBY: Bonjour.

BESSIE: He's very shy.

JANE: Bessie, how is Mrs Reed?

BESSIE: Well she wasn't too bad when I wrote you. The doctors said she had a good few months…years perhaps, but…

JANE: What Bessie? What has happened?

BESSIE: It's Master John. He's passed away.

71

JANE: Master John? How?

BESSIE: He lived rough and wild in that London, Jane. He got into debt and into jail. Mrs Reed bailed him out more than once, but whenever he got free he just went back to his old habits. They found him in his rooms down there. They say it was suicide!

JANE: How does his mother bear it?

BESSIE: At first I thought the shock would kill her. But she rallied a little. She keeps asking for you.

JANE: Why me?

BESSIE: She says she can't rest until she sees you. Let me take you to her. She's in the Red Room.

SCENE FOUR
AUNT REED DIES

AUNT REED is sleeping in a wheelchair. JANE enters and she wakes up.

AUNT REED: Who is that?

JANE: It is me, Mrs Reed.

AUNT REED: Who are you? I know that voice. Who calls?

JANE: Jane Eyre.

AUNT REED: Are you Jane Eyre?

JANE: I am.

AUNT REED: You were born to torment me. I curse the day my husband placed the nasty little cuckoo in my nest. I would never have done such things but for you.

JANE: I should leave you to rest Mrs Reed.

AUNT REED: Rest? I cannot rest. Are you Jane Eyre?

JANE: I am.

AUNT REED: Where is John? My beautiful baby John...there is no good in bleeding me for money. There is no money left.

JANE: Can I get you some water Mrs Reed?

AUNT REED grabs her hand.

AUNT REED: There is something I have to tell you. Is anyone else there?

JANE: No. We are quite alone.

AUNT REED: I have twice done you wrong Jane Eyre. I broke the promise I made to my husband to bring you up as my own.

JANE: And the other?

AUNT REED: There is a letter that concerns you. Go to my dressing case. There's a box. Open it...inside...the letter... read it.

JANE takes a letter out of the dressing case.

JANE: Madam, will you have the goodness to send me the address of my niece, Jane Eyre? As my only living relative, I wish to write to her at the earliest opportunity. It is my dying wish to make contact with my brother's only child. I am madam etc etc. William Eyre, Madeira. This was five years ago. Why did I never hear of it?

AUNT REED: I wrote back that December. I told him you had died of a fever at Lowood. Leave me now.

JANE: Why do you hate me so?

AUNT REED: Gateshead was never the same after you infected this house. Your nature is bad. I shall never forget that day you turned on me, like an animal.

JANE: I was a child.

AUNT REED: I wish you had died.

JANE: Love me then, or hate me, Aunt Reed, as you will. You have my full and free forgiveness.

AUNT REED dies. She steps out of the wheelchair and goes down into the trap.

Music. JANE puts up her coat and picks up her bag as BESSIE returns.

BESSIE: I made you something for't journey.

JANE: Oh Bessie, thankyou.

BESSIE: You'll let me know your address won't you? When you find yourself a new post.

JANE: I will.

BESSIE: I wish you well. Goodbye Miss Jane.

They hug each other goodbye.

JANE: Goodbye box hedge, goodbye wet lawn, goodbye Gateshead.

JANE exits along the gantry as the scene transforms back to Hay Lane.

SCENE FIVE
HAY LANE

Music. JANE returns to the platform. BERTHA can be heard singing as she sits on the edge of the platform looking out. ROCHESTER enters with PILOT.

ROCHESTER: Jane Eyre! How very like you to walk all the way from Millcote and not send for the trap. I should've known that if I took a stroll down Hay Lane you would pop up from somewhere. Pilot! Down! You've been away a whole month. Doing what, I wonder?

JANE: I've been with my aunt, sir, who is dead.

ROCHESTER: A true Janian reply.

JANE climbs down the ladder.

JANE: How was London, sir?

ROCHESTER: How do you know I've been in London?

JANE: Mrs Fairfax told me in a letter.

ROCHESTER: Oh. My tailor is now a wealthy man. The problem with expensive attire is you have to live up to it. Fairy that you are, you don't have a potion in that bag of yours to turn me into a handsome man?

JANE: That would be past the power of magic, sir. *(PILOT runs to JANE and she pats him for a moment.)* Tell me sir, have you been making enquiries regarding a new situation for me?

ROCHESTER: I have not been neglecting my duties. Adele is running rings round Mrs Fairfax and being a damned nuisance. Go on up to the house. Well, go on!

JANE: Sir.

ROCHESTER: Pilot!

JANE exits. ROCHESTER watches her go.

SCENE SIX
HOME TO THORNFIELD

ADELE runs up the ramp and along the gantry to the platform carrying a bunch of flowers. She thinks about the best place to put them in JANE's room. MRS FAIRFAX follows a little while after. They meet on the gantry.

ADELE: Oh Mrs Fairfax, I will put them in her room.

FAIRFAX: Yes and I will see if they still have water.

ADELE shows her where they are.

ADELE: There. I will go and see if she has come.

ADELE runs back the way she came while MRS FAIRFAX tidies up the flowers.

JANE enters.

ADELE: Oh Miss Eyre!

JANE: Hello.

ADELE: You must come up to your room, I have picked some flowers for you. Mrs Fairfax! She is there!

FAIRFAX: Oh Jane, I am glad you are back. I'm sorry for your loss.

They embrace.

ADELE: There are the flowers I have picked. Take off your jacket. I will help. You are staying yes? I will help you unpack your bag.

JANE: There might be something in there for you.

ADELE discovers a package in the bag.

ADELE: Un cadeau! Merci!

She unwraps a gingerbread man.

ADELE: Ah! Mr Rochester.

She bites the head off. She offers JANE a piece.

ADELE: For you.

ADELE jumps up and runs out on to the gantry.

ADELE: You must come there is an ants' nest I want to show you.

Music. Time passing. JANE, MRS FAIRFAX and ADELE are sewing in the parlour. PILOT dozes at their feet.

JANE: When did the Ingrams leave Mrs Fairfax?

FAIRFAX: They set out for London a few days ago.

JANE: I suppose everything is settled between the master and Miss Ingram?

FAIRFAX: I'm sure it is all in hand. I suspect Miss Ingram is amongst the bright lights picking out her trousseau, though I've no doubt that I will be the last to be informed of the date.

ROCHESTER enters.

ROCHESTER: Good evening. Don't get up Mrs Fairfax.

FAIRFAX: Can I get you anything sir?

ROCHESTER: No I was just looking for Pilot. Come on dog.

ROCHESTER and PILOT exit. Music. BERTHA sings. They swap positions. Time passing.

JANE: Mrs Fairfax, I saw Mr Rochester take his horse out this afternoon.

FAIRFAX: He had business in Millcote. I asked him if he'd be looking in on his tailor while he was there. He's having a new suit made. It must be the wedding outfit. It must be!

They change positions again. More time passing.

JANE: Who called at the house this morning?

FAIRFAX: One of the Ingram's staff brought a letter from Miss Blanche. A love note I've no doubt. The announcement is imminent. I can feel it in my bones.

SCENE SEVEN
THE PROPOSAL

ROCHESTER is on the platform. He gets distracted by a moth and gets it onto his hand. He calls down to JANE to look at it.

ROCHESTER: Jane. Here. Come and look at this little chap. There. Look at his wings. Thornfield is a pleasant place in summer isn't it?

JANE: Yes sir.

ROCHESTER: You have become attached to the house?

JANE: Yes.

ROCHESTER: It's always the way. No sooner have you settled somewhere than a voice calls out to you to rise and move on.

JANE: Must I move on sir?

ROCHESTER: I believe you must. I've found a place that might suit. A family in Ireland.

JANE: That's a long way off.

ROCHESTER: No matter. A girl of your sense will not object to the distance or the voyage.

JANE: Not the voyage, but the distance. The sea is a barrier –

ROCHESTER: From what, Jane?

JANE: From England…from Thornfield… From *you*, sir.

ROCHESTER: We have been good friends, haven't we?

JANE: Yes, sir.

ROCHESTER: I sometimes have a strange feeling with regards to you. It is as if I had a string, tied somewhere under my left ribs, tightly knotted to a similar string situated in the same part of your little frame. If the land and sea came between us I am afraid that string would be snapped and I would take to bleeding inwardly and you would forget me.

JANE: That I never would sir, you know.

Bird song.

ROCHESTER: Jane. Listen to that.

JANE: I wish I'd never come here.

ROCHESTER: Do not say such things.

JANE: I love Thornfield. I love it because I have lived in it a full and delightful life. I have not been trampled on. I have not been petrified. I have talked face to face with what I most delight in, an original, vigorous, expanded mind. I have known you Mr Rochester. And it strikes me with terror that I absolutely must be torn from you forever. I see the necessity of departure and it is like looking on the necessity of death.

ROCHESTER: Where do you see the necessity?

JANE: Where? In the shape of Miss Ingram, your bride.

ROCHESTER: I have no bride!

JANE: But you will have.

ROCHESTER: Yes I will.

JANE: Then I must go. You said so yourself.

ROCHESTER: No! You must stay!

JANE: Stay? Do you think I can stay to become nothing to you? Do you think I am an automaton? A machine without feelings? Do you think because I am poor, obscure, plain and little, that I am soulless and heartless? You think wrong! I have as much heart as you and full as much soul. And if God had gifted me with some beauty and much wealth I would have made it as hard for you to leave me as it is now for me to leave you. I am not talking to you through custom, convention or even of mortal flesh. It is my spirit that addresses your spirit, as if we had both passed through the grave and stood now at God's feet, equal. As we are!

ROCHESTER: As we are, Jane!

ROCHESTER grabs hold of her.

JANE: Let me go! Let me go!

ROCHESTER: Jane, don't struggle so. Jane!

JANE moves away up the ramp and on to the gantry.

ROCHESTER: You are like a frantic bird tearing at its own feathers!

JANE: I am no bird and no net ensnares me. I am a free human being with an independent will that I now exert to leave you.

ROCHESTER: Jane! Jane! Marry me!

JANE: Do you mock me?

ROCHESTER: Do you doubt me?

JANE: Entirely. Your bride stands between us.

ROCHESTER: I would not – I could not – marry Miss Ingram.
I have no love for her. You! You I love as my own flesh.
You. Poor, obscure, plain and little as you are. Marry me.

JANE: Me?

ROCHESTER: Say yes, quickly.

ROCHESTER climbs the ladder to JANE.

JANE: Let me look at your face. Turn to the light.

ROCHESTER: Why?

JANE: I want to read your countenance.

She gets hold of him and closely examines his face.

JANE: Are you in earnest? Do you truly love me? Do you
sincerely wish me to be your wife?

ROCHESTER: I do. I swear it.

JANE: Then I will marry you.

They kiss on the ladder. JANE climbs down. ROCHESTER leaves.

SCENE EIGHT
THE RIPPING OF THE VEIL

*MRS FAIRFAX enters down the ramp and meets JANE as she comes down
the ladder.*

FAIRFAX: I feel so astonished I hardly know what to say.
I swear not five minutes ago Mr Rochester came in and
said you were to be married.

JANE: Yes. He has said the same thing to me.

FAIRFAX: No doubt it is true since you say so, but how
it will answer I cannot tell. You are so young and so
little acquainted with men. Be on your guard. Distrust

yourself as well as him. Gentlemen in his station are not accustomed to marry their governesses.

Music. ROCHESTER and JANE take up different positions around the stage for each of the wedding preparation vignettes.

ROCHESTER: You can't get married in those boots.

JANE: What's wrong with them?

ROCHESTER: They're old boots. No one gets married in old boots.

JANE: I can sir, and I will.

They move to a new position for the second vignette.

ROCHESTER: I've ordered Chinese silk from London Jane. It will make a beautiful wedding dress.

JANE: I will use my own salary to furnish my wardrobe thank you sir. You may keep the silk to make yourself an infinite series of waistcoats.

The ensemble enter carrying a box. They walk around the stage passing it between them, finally giving it to JANE. She opens the box and finds the veil.

ROCHESTER: Jane. I have something for you. This will make you look like a Princess.

JANE: Why? Because it will hide my face? It must have cost a fortune.

ROCHESTER: Of course it did. Please. You must accept one gift from your intended. And every bride must have a veil.

JANE: Very well. I will wear it. But only because it makes you happy.

Music. BERTHA sings. The ensemble pull the veil out of the box. They clip it onto JANE's head and she climbs the ladder with it flowing behind her. As she stands on the platform fans are used to waft the veil out over the stage, making it fly above JANE's head. It is then whipped away. JANE is left alone on the platform.

JANE: Who's there?? Who's there?

ROCHESTER enters.

ROCHESTER: Jane! Everything is prepared. Tomorrow we set out for London as soon as we return from the church. What's the matter?

JANE: I passed a strange night sir. I dreamed Thornfield was a dreary ruin. I climbed like some spectral fiend up the crumbling walls, cobwebs trailing from me like a shroud.

ROCHESTER: It was just a dream Jane. The house is intact and you are no fiend. By the end of the week we will be in Marseilles.

JANE: That is not the end of it, sir. When I woke, or so I thought, a light dazzled me. Through it I could see a shadow, in the shape of a woman, standing in my room. This was not a woman from the house, sir, this was not Mrs Fairfax, this was not even Grace Poole. It was some other woman and she wore my wedding veil as she stood before the mirror. Then she took the veil from her head and she tore it in two. The candle was blown out. Was that a dream sir?

ROCHESTER: Of course it was. What else could it have been?

JANE: The thing is, sir, when I got up and went to draw the curtains, there was the veil, …in two pieces, lying on the floor.

The ensemble become the voices in JANE's head. They climb the ladders on either side of the platform. They hand one piece of the veil to ROCHESTER. JANE hands him the other half.

ROCHESTER: This was half dream, half reality. A woman did enter your room and that woman was, must have been, Grace Poole.

JANE: This was not Grace Poole.

ROCHESTER: There is no other possible explanation. I know you wonder why I keep such a woman in the house. Of course you do. But I have my reasons. When we have been married for a year and a day I will tell you. Will you trust me, Jane?

The ensemble become the voices in JANE's head.

VOICE: A year and a day?

VOICE: You cannot be satisfied with that.

VOICE: You know what you saw.

VOICE: Why can't he tell you now?

VOICE: You cannot be satisfied.

VOICE: That woman was not Grace Poole.

VOICE: Are you really going to wait for a year and a day?

VOICE: You cannot be satisfied.

The ensemble repeat their protestations until JANE silences them.

JANE: Enough!

JANE kisses ROCHESTER.

SCENE NINE
WEDDING DRESS

The ensemble surround JANE on the platform.

One of the band sings 'Who stole your crown.'

> *She was young, wild fire eyes a-gleaming*
> *Lost on the Western wind*
> *By the hands of love she was bound and blinded*
> *To her final end*

> *Who stole your crown?*
> *While your back was turned*
> *Bow your head down*
> *While your body slowly....*

> *So she held her breath for one word of kindness*
> *The truth she learned too late*

Heaven and the Earth turned upon their axis
The smoke it suffocates

Who stole your crown?
While your back was turned
Bow your head down
While your body slowly....

Once a lie's believed you can't stop it spreading
It breaks across the bow
You can't turn around though you know where you're heading
Nothing matters now

Who stole your crown?
While your back was turned
Bow your head down
While your body slowly burns

JANE looks in the mirror. She unbuttons the dress she is wearing.

The ensemble help her to take it off and place it on a hanger that has been flown in. They mirror her moves as she tries tying up her hair. She changes her mind and lets it back down. She lifts up her skirt and looks at her boots. Her wedding dress flies in as the old dress flies out. The ensemble help her to get into her wedding dress. They mirror her movements as she does a slow twirl whilst looking in the mirror.

The ensemble leave. ROCHESTER goes up to the platform.

ROCHESTER: Not so poor and plain after all. Mrs Fairfax?

FAIRFAX: Yes sir?

ROCHESTER: Have the carriages brought round to the front of the house. We shall be leaving direct from the church.

ADELE: Oh Miss Eyre! Oh you look so beautiful in your dress.

ROCHESTER: Not now, Adele. Goodbye Mrs Fairfax.

ADELE and MRS FAIRFAX wave them goodbye.

SCENE TEN
WEDDING INTERRUPTED

ROCHESTER takes JANE's hand and pulls her along the gantry and down the ramp into the church. The REVEREND stands on the platform ready to lead the marriage service.

REV: In the presence of God, Father, Son and Holy Spirit, we have come together to witness the marriage of Edward Fairfax Rochester and Jane Eyre. Marriage is a way of life made holy by God, and blessed by the presence of our Lord Jesus Christ. I am required to charge of you both that if either of you knows of any impediment why you may not be lawfully joined together in matrimony that you confess it now.

No reply.

REV: Wilt thou take this woman for thy wedded wife?

The LAWYER enters and interrupts.

LAWYER: This marriage cannot go on. I declare the existence of an impediment.

ROCHESTER: Proceed.

REV: Sir, I cannot proceed until I have established the truth or falsehood of this objection.

LAWYER: I am in a position to prove my allegation unequivocally.

ROCHESTER: Who are you?

LAWYER: My name is Briggs. I'm a solicitor from London. Mr Rochester has a wife, now living.

ROCHESTER: Proceed!

LAWYER: I have here a record of marriage from St James' church in Spanish Town, Jamaica. It was there Mr Rochester married one Bertha Antoinetta Mason some fifteen years ago.

ROCHESTER: This proves I had a wife it doesn't prove she is still living.

LAWYER: I have a witness to the fact.

ROCHESTER: Produce him or be damned.

MASON enters.

MASON: Hello Edward.

ROCHESTER: What have you to say? What have you to say!?

ROCHESTER climbs up the ladder aggressively heading for MASON.

MASON: Bertha Rochester, his wife, lives now at Thornfield Hall. I saw her there last April. I am her brother.

ROCHESTER: Enough! There will be no wedding today. You are fifteen years too late! What these gentlemen say is true. I have a wife. Bertha Mason is now living at Thornfield. A lunatic, who would burn you as you slept. Come up to the house and let me introduce you to my wife.

SCENE ELEVEN
MEETING BERTHA

The ensemble take positions around the stage staring up at BERTHA on the platform as the V/O soundtrack plays. BERTHA hums 'Orphan Child' to herself.

GRACE (V/O): Sometimes she is raving with fury, at other times she presents a dejected look, a fixed absent stare and a deep melancholy. If she gets in possession of any kind of knife, scissors, tools, whatever, then she will use it for injury. Proper instruments of restraint are necessary in order to maintain control. Everything must be removed from her reach by which she might possibly injure herself and others. Bar all the windows. She will jump if she can.

ROCHESTER: I have to see her Grace.

GRACE: Take care sire, for God's sake take care!

ROCHESTER: This is my wife.

BERTHA sings. JANE journeys up the ramp to the platform where BERTHA waits for her holding the old grey dress. They face each other for a moment and JANE takes the dress from BERTHA.

SCENE TWELVE
BERTHA'S STORY

ROCHESTER is collapsed on the ramp. BERTHA sings.

His coming was my hope
His parting was my pain
The truest love in my heart
Was ice in every vein

I dreamed it would be endless bliss
As I loved, loved to be
And to this I did press
As blind as eagerly

JANE comes down the ladder.

ROCHESTER: Jane. I've been here all night, Jane. I could hear nothing. Talk to me. Speak.

JANE: I need some water.

ROCHESTER fetches her water. They sit down together at the bottom of the platform.

ROCHESTER: How are you now?

JANE: Everything around me is changed. I must change too.

ROCHESTER: I will change everything Jane. I'll lock up Thornfield Hall. I'll nail the door shut and bar the lower windows. And I will pay Grace Poole two hundred a year to live here with that lunatic, that demented creature.

JANE: Why? Why do you speak of your wife with such hatred? It is vindictive and cruel. She cannot help the way she is.

ROCHESTER: It is not because she is mad that I hate her.
If you were mad do you think I would hate you?

JANE: Yes, I do.

BERTHA sings.

> *Haunted as a path*
> *Through wilderness and wood*
> *Might and woe and wrath*
> *Between our spirits stood*
>
> *Fire that burns in my eyes*
> *Anger grows beneath my cries*
> *My soul was lost my sorrow died*
> *A long time ago*

ROCHESTER: I was twenty-one, Jane, and sent half way
across the world to marry a bride already courted for me.
Thirty thousand pounds was the price my father secured
in exchange for my future happiness. She dazzled me at
first. I thought I loved her. We were married. She began to
have outbursts of violence. Vices sprang up fast and rank.
A doctor declared her mad. Doors were locked, windows
barred. No servant could bear it. I could not bear it, but
she was my wife. Only cruelty would check her behavior
and I would not use cruelty.

> *And so the demons in my head*
> *Play freely with my every breath*
> *And stoke the flames of my despair*
> *My rage, my rage, my death*
>
> *In the night they crawl*
> *They fight, they kick, they scream*
> *Breaking me apart*
> *tearing at the seams.*

ROCHESTER: One night, woken by her cries, I thought 'this
life is hell.' I took a pistol from my trunk meaning to shoot
myself. But a wind blew through my casement. A breeze
from Europe. And a new thought resolved in my mind. Go

home. To England. Take her to Thornfield. Have her cared for. But let her identity and her marriage to you be buried in oblivion. Shelter her degradation with secrecy and leave her.

> *My love has sworn with sealing kiss*
> *With me to live to die*
> *I have at last my endless bliss*
> *As I love, loved am I*

ROCHESTER: To say that I have a wife is an empty mockery Jane. I should not have deceived you. Live with me as my wife. Accept my pledge of fidelity and give me yours. Why are you silent? You understand what I am asking of you? All I want is this promise: 'I will be yours Mr Rochester.'

JANE: I will not be yours.

ROCHESTER: Jane, do you mean to go one way in the world while I go another?

JANE: I do.

He holds her.

ROCHESTER: Jane. Do you mean it now?

JANE: I do.

He kisses her.

ROCHESTER: And now?

JANE: I do.

ROCHESTER: What shall I do, Jane?

JANE: You will forget me long before I forget you.

ROCHESTER grabs her throat.

ROCHESTER: You make me a liar with that language. Never was anything so frail and yet so indomitable. I could bend her with my finger and thumb, but what good would it do if I bent her, if I crushed her? It is you, spirit, Jane, that I want.

JANE: I am going sir.

ROCHESTER: Jane.

JANE: Mr Rochester.

JANE walks away.

SCENE THIRTEEN
LEAVING THORNFIELD

The ensemble enter the space looking at JANE. ROCHESTER slumps down by the platform as JANE slowly climbs the ladder. Half way up she leans out as far as she can, looking up and down. She runs along the gantry and down the ramp. The ensemble join in fleeing from Thornfield. They all gather together to form a coach.

JANE: Where is this coach going? How much does it cost? Take me as far as you can for twenty shillings. I have no more.

The coach stops and they all fall to the floor. A moment of looking out – watching the coach leave. The ensemble look around – 'where am I?'

They look in different directions before all turning to look at JANE.

JANE approaches one of the ensemble standing on the platform.

JANE: What work do people do here? What is the trade?

MAN: Farm labouring. Or needle factory.

JANE: Do they employ women?

MAN: No.

JANE comes down the ladder and crosses to another ensemble member.

JANE: Would you give me some money for my leather boots?

WOMAN: What would I want with a pair of old boots.

JANE: Would you give me some bread for them?

WOMAN: I don't deal with beggars in this shop.

A clap of thunder. Lightening. Rain falls. JANE looks to the heavens.

JANE: Helen. Will I see you again when I die?

She sits down on the ramp, then collapses.

SCENE FOURTEEN
MOOR HOUSE

ST JOHN enters and finds JANE collapsed on the ramp. He checks her breathing and then tries to lift her up.

ST JOHN: Can you hear me? What is your name? Diana! Diana! Fetch water.

DIANA brings water.

DIANA: Here.

ST JOHN gives JANE some water.

ST JOHN: Help me get her in.

The song begins as they help JANE up. Solo voice. Elvis Presley's 'He Knows Just What I Need'.

> *My Jesus knows when I am lonely*
> *He knows each pain, he sees each tear…*
>
> *My Jesus Knows repeat as 'Oohs' (Verse)*

They place JANE on the ramp as if in a bed. They take off her boots and put a blanket over her. DIANA sits beside her and mops her brow. ST JOHN kneels and prays. JANE sits up slowly and ST JOHN stands.

DIANA: What's your name?

JANE: Jane Eyre.

DIANA brings in a stool and a crucifix and sets up their home as ST JOHN reads aloud from the Bible. As he does so JANE slowly comes round. DIANA invites her to sit and gives her a bowl of soup.

ST JOHN: In you, Lord, I have taken refuge;
let me never be put to shame;
come quickly to my rescue;
be my rock of refuge,

a strong fortress to save me.
Since you are my rock and my fortress,
for the sake of your name lead and guide me.
Keep me free from the trap that is set for me.
For you are my refuge.
Into your hands I commit my spirit.
So deliver me Lord
My faithful God
Amen.

DIANA: Amen.

JANE sits and eats her soup.

DIANA: You must be careful and not eat too quickly. You have
had a fever for three days.

JANE: I hope I shall not eat long at your expense.

ST JOHN: When you have indicated to us the residence of your
friends you may be restored to them.

JANE: I must tell you plainly, I am absolutely without home or
friends.

ST JOHN: Where did you last reside?

JANE: That must remain my secret.

DIANA: Which in my opinion she has every right to keep.
You may rely on our discretion.

ST JOHN: There is nothing covered, that shall not be revealed;
neither hid, that shall not be known.

DIANA: St John, you are too inquisitive. Let her be at peace a
while.

ST JOHN: If I know nothing about her or her history then I
cannot help her. And you need help, do you not?

JANE: You and your sister have done me a great service.
But I do not wish to rely on your charity. Show me where to
work, where to earn enough to keep myself. Then I will go.

DIANA: You'll have a few more bowls of beef tea before you
go anywhere.

ST JOHN: My sister would have pleasure in keeping you. I feel
more inclination to put you in way of keeping yourself.
But you must be aware as a poor clergyman my sphere is
narrow. My help will be of the humblest sort.

JANE: I will be a servant or a plain workwoman, if I can be no
better.

ST JOHN: If such is your spirit then I will do my very best to
help you in my own time and way.

DIANA: And in the meantime you will stay here with us.

*The band begin singing Elvis Presley's 'He Knows Just What I
Need' as ST JOHN and DIANA help JANE transform the stage into
the schoolroom.*

SCENE FIFTEEN
JANE BEGINS TEACHING

*They place books on the ramp. JANE and ST JOHN occasionally glance
at each other as they do so. The ensemble sitting with the band become
a class of children waiting to start their lessons. They sit down ready to
learn. ST JOHN leaves before the end of the song.*

DIANA: Do you have everything you need?

JANE: Apart from my pupils.

DIANA: They will be here soon enough.

JANE: It was very kind of Mr Rivers to find me this post.

DIANA: These children have never been educated. And then
we found you at the door to our home. The Lord has a
plan for us all Jane.

JANE: The Lord is a loving tyrant.

DIANA: Hardships are many and various and you have had
    your troubles to bear I think.

JANE: And they find their ease here Diana. And I am grateful.

DIANA leaves and JANE turns to the class.

JANE: Good morning children.

CHILDREN: Good morning Miss.

JANE: Put down you slates and gather round. *(JANE reads.)* That
    punctual servant of all work, the sun, had just risen, and
    begun to strike a light on the morning of the thirteenth
    of May, one thousand eight hundred and twenty-seven,
    when Mr. Samuel Pickwick burst like another sun from his
    slumbers, threw open his chamber window, and looked out
    upon the world beneath.

JANE moves to a stool at the end of the ramp. ST JOHN enters.

ST JOHN: How have you found your first week? Harder than
    expected?

JANE: On the contrary. My young scholars have pleased me.

ST JOHN: The village is ablaze with talk of Miss Eyre. But perhaps
    your accommodation, your furniture has disappointed your
    expectations. They are in truth scanty enough.

JANE: It is clean and comfortable. And I'm not such a fool as
    to regret the absence of a carpet and a sofa.

ST JOHN: What you left before I met you of course I do not
    know. But I counsel you to resist firmly every temptation to
    look back.

JANE: That is what I mean to do St John.

ST JOHN: A year ago I myself was intensely miserable.
    I thought I had made a mistake in entering the ministry.
    Its uniform duties wearied me to death. But my powers

heard a call from heaven to rise. God has an errand for me: to labour as a missionary in India.

JANE: The parlour is not your sphere. You choose a harder life than I.

ST JOHN: Jane is not such a weakling as you would make out. She can bear a mountain blast as well as any of us. I've watched you sit alone here after class. What is it you study?

JANE: I am learning German.

ST JOHN: I see you are committed to your studies. I have much to learn about India. Will you aid me in my preparations?

JANE: I owe you that much and more.

ST JOHN: I want you to give up German and learn Hindustani.

JANE: You are not an easy man to refuse, St John.

ST JOHN: Good. It is settled then. I will come here to the school room for an hour or two at the end of each day. We can start tomorrow.

JANE and ST JOHN study alongside one another. Members of the ensemble take their books and give them new ones in time with the music.

SCENE SIXTEEN
ST JOHN PROPOSES

Time has passed.

JANE: I almost begin to regret that I will never have cause to use this language, after such labours.

ST JOHN: Indeed?

JANE: I would succumb to a fever within a month in such a hot clime.

ST JOHN: Jane you know it's only six weeks till I leave.

JANE: God will protect you for you have undertaken his work.

ST JOHN: I go as God's servant to leave behind a life of selfish ease and barren obscurity. It seems strange to me that all do not burn to do the same.

JANE: All have not your powers St John. It would be folly for the weak to march with the strong.

ST JOHN: I do not speak to the feeble Jane. Come with me to India. Come as my fellow labourer. God and nature intended you for a missionary's wife.

JANE: I am not fit for it. I have no vocation.

ST JOHN: Who is fit for it? Humble as I am I can give you the aid you want. I can stand by you always, help you from moment to moment.

JANE: But my powers for this undertaking? Where are they? I cannot feel them.

ST JOHN: Well then I have an answer for you – hear it. Jane, I have watched you these past ten months and I am certain you were sent for a purpose. Jane, you are diligent, faithful, constant, and very gentle. I can trust you unreservedly. Will you come with me?

JANE: I cannot answer you now. Will you let me think?

ST JOHN: Very willingly.

SCENE SEVENTEEN
JANE CONSIDERS THE PROPOSAL

JANE walks up the ramp as some of the ensemble appear as the voices in her head.

VOICE: I can cross oceans with him.

VOICE: We could labour under the Eastern sun.

DIANA enters and offers her thoughts to JANE.

DIANA: Jane I know he can be as inexorable as death. He is driven by forces stronger than himself. You inspire him Jane. Since you arrived the flame of his faith burns brighter than ever. And remember you have very little of your own. He would give you a home, a life, work which satisfies you. The wise woman builds her house, but the foolish one with her own hands tears it down. I only wish what's best for you. Have faith. God will guide you.

DIANA exits.

SCENE EIGHTEEN
JANE REJECTS THE PROPOSAL

JANE has come to a decision. She calls out to ST JOHN.

JANE: I will go to India with you. If I may go free.

ST JOHN: Your answer is not clear.

JANE: You and Diana have been as brother and sister to me. Let us continue as such.

ST JOHN: I already have a sister. Our union must be consecrated by marriage. You have said you will go with me to India, remember that.

JANE: Conditionally.

ST JOHN: I want a wife. Someone I can influence efficiently in life and retain absolutely till death.

JANE: Seek one elsewhere St John, one fitted to you.

ST JOHN: One fitted to my purpose you mean. I tell you it is not the insignificant private individual I wish to mate, it is the missionary.

JANE: And I will give the missionary my energies, but not my self.

ST JOHN: Do you think God will be satisfied with half an offering? It is under God's standard that I enlist you. I cannot accept on his behalf a divided allegiance. It must be entire.

JANE: I repeat: I will go with you willingly as a fellow missionary, but not as your wife.

ST JOHN: I repeat: we must be married.

JANE: Oh St John, have mercy.

ST JOHN: If I listened to human pride I would say no more to you of marriage, but I listen to my duty. Undoubtedly enough of love would follow our marriage to render the union acceptable. If you reject this, it is not me you reject, but God.

SCENE NINETEEN
JANE DECIDES

ST JOHN preaches as JANE listens. The voices crowd in on JANE.

ST JOHN: Man is not the centre of all things. The duty of every man and woman and child is to live for the glory of God. Listen not to human pride. Let duty, honour and perseverance be your guide and do all things for the glory of God.

VOICE: In leaving England, I leave an empty land – for what can Mr Rochester ever be to me now?

JANE: Yes, my duty now is to forget him, not to drag on from day to day, waiting for some impossible change to reunite us.

VOICE: Forget impossible change. Remember what St John can offer. A new life, a home, a family.

ST JOHN: Sacrifice your own desires. Glad hearted obedience glorifies great wisdom and is not a burden.

JANE: Yet would it not be strange to be chained for life to a man who regarded one only as a useful tool?

VOICE: St. John is good and clever.

ST JOHN: Humility is the foundation of Christian virtue.

VOICE: He prizes my character with a clear eye.

JANE: He prizes me as a soldier would a good weapon.

VOICE: St John is good and clever.

VOICE: Mr Rochester is not here.

VOICES: The case is very plain.

JANE: Can I bear it?

VOICES: *(All.)* Yes.

ST JOHN: They that overcome will inherit all. God will wipe away every tear from their eyes. May God give you the strength to choose that better part which will never be taken from you.

JANE stands and moves to the ramp. She hears ROCHESTER's voice.

ROCHESTER: Jane. Jane.

ST JOHN: What have you seen? What have you heard?

JANE: St John, I cannot do it.

ROCHESTER: Jane!

JANE climbs the tallest ladder to listen.

SCENE FOURTEEN
RETURN TO THORNFIELD

JANE stands on the platform. Ash drops from the sky. The broken windows of Thornfield litter the space.

JANE: Thornfield!

JANE explores the space. BERTHA sings 'Crazy' by Gnarls Barkley.

MRS FAIRFAX enters.

> *Does that make me crazy?*
> *Possibly.*

FAIRFAX: Jane?

JANE: Mrs Fairfax.

BERTHA and the ensemble set fire to the buckets.

MRS. FAIRFAX: You could see the flames for miles they say. That poor woman. Turns it out it was her that set fire to the master's bed that time. This time she set the whole place alight. The master was very brave, he got us all out. But he couldn't find her, and then we saw her up on the roof. And he would go back in for her. But she jumped. God rest her soul.

Reprise of 'Crazy'.

JANE: And Mr Rochester?

MRS FAIRFAX: He was still inside when the house collapsed. But they got him out; he survived.

JANE: And where is he now?

MRS FAIRFAX: I've been looking after him down at the Lodge. I'll take you to him.

The fire buckets are extinguished.

Bird song. ROCHESTER enters slowly down the ramp. He is now blind.

He pauses at the bottom of the ramp, sensing the outside world.

PILOT runs past him. ROCHESTER sits slowly on a stool at the corner of the platform with PILOT lying near to him. JANE enters from under the platform.

PILOT wags his tail, barks and runs to her.

ROCHESTER: Pilot! Pilot!

PILOT sits beside JANE.

ROCHESTER: Who is that? Mrs Fairfax?

JANE kneels beside ROCHESTER and touches his hand. He pulls away, then holds both her hands. Then touches her face.

ROCHESTER: Are you real?

JANE: I am come back to you sir.

They stand and embrace

JANE: It's a bright sunny day. The rain is over and gone.

They kiss.

BERTHA sings a verse from 'the Orphan child.'

> *The mountains stand before me*
> *The rivers running wild*
> *The wind it howls, the rain it falls*
> *Upon this orphan child*

The ensemble slowly enter as ROCHESTER takes off his coat, which is then formed into a baby as in the opening of Act One. He hands the baby to JANE.

VOICE: It's a girl

VOICE: It's a girl

VOICE: It's a girl

VOICE: It's a girl

ROCHESTER: It's a girl.

Blackout.

The end.